P9-DCD-666

Charlie Joe Jackson's Guide to Printing Money

Wait, isn't that illegal?

Also by Tommy Greenwald

Charlie Joe Jackson's Guide to Not Reading
Charlie Joe Jackson's Guide to Extra Credit
Charlie Joe Jackson's Guide to Summer Vacation
Jack Strong Takes a Stand

Tommy Greenwald

Charlie Joe Jackson's Guide to

I make money the old-fashioned way...

...by doing as little work as possible.

Making Money

Illustrations by J.P. Coovert

Roaring Brook Press ✳ New York

Text copyright © 2014 by Tommy Greenwald
Illustrations copyright © 2014 by J.P. Coovert
Published by Roaring Brook Press

Roaring Brook Press is a division of Holtzbrinck Publishing Holdings Limited Partnership
175 Fifth Avenue, New York, New York 10010
mackids.com

Library of Congress Cataloging-in-Publication Data

Greenwald, Tom.
    Charlie Joe Jackson's guide to making money / Tommy Greenwald ; illustrated by J.P. Coovert.
— First edition.
      pages cm
    Summary : "When his weekly allowance just isn't cutting it anymore, lovable slacker Charlie Joe devises
ways to make more money—and fast"—Provided by publisher.
    ISBN 978-1-59643-840-8 (hardback)—ISBN 978-1-59643-842-2 (ebook)
    [1. Moneymaking projects—Fiction.   2. Middle schools—Fiction.   3. Schools—Fiction.   4. Humorous
stories.]   I. Coovert, J. P., illustrator.   II. Title.
    PZ7.G8523Cgo 2014
    [Fic]—dc23
                                                                                2013044997

Roaring Brook Press books may be purchased for business or promotional use. For information on bulk
purchases please contact Macmillan Corporate and Premium Sales Department at (800) 221-7945 x5442
or by e-mail at specialmarkets@macmillan.com.

First edition 2014
Book design by Andrew Arnold
Printed in the United States of America by RR Donnelley & Sons Company, Harrisonburg, Virginia

10 9 8 7 6 5 4 3 2 1

In memory of Moose

"A perfectly nice dog."

INTRODUCTION

I like money.

I *don't* like working hard.

It turns out that's a problem.

Who knew?

It's not like I'm greedy or anything like that (I swear). It just so happened that last year, I needed money, and I needed to figure out a way to make some.

Fast.

Without working hard.

You know what I learned? It's possible. It can be done. I know, because I did it.

Sure, a couple of minor things might have gone wrong along the way.

But so what?

That's part of the fun, right?

Part One
THE DOG AND THE GOPHER

First, a little background.

I discovered the joy of money when I was little, and my parents gave me and my older sister, Megan, an allowance. Like a dollar a week—nothing major, but enough for candy, or soda, or the occasional slice of pizza when Megan would take me downtown.

In return, we were expected to do one thing: stay alive.

But then, when we started getting a little bit older, my parents—especially my mom—expected more for their money. It was small stuff, for sure: Brush my teeth for a full minute, put my clothes away (by balling them up and stuffing them in a drawer, but Mom didn't have to know that), feed the dogs—that kind of thing.

Megan—whose only imperfection was that she was perfect—handled the new responsibilities without complaining at all.

I, on the other hand, wanted a raise. I think I was about seven years old when I finally got brave enough to bring it up.

"Mom," I said one day while pretending to fold a pair of socks, "can we start getting five dollars a week? Look at all this stuff we're doing now."

She looked at me. "What are you going to do with five dollars a week?"

"There's lots of things I could do with five dollars," I said. "Like take you and Dad out to dinner, for example. I would totally do that."

Pretty quick thinking for seven, huh?

Mom laughed, then took the socks from my hand and opened the drawer to put them in.

"Wait!" I shouted, but it was too late. She stared down in horror at the war zone of wrinkled clothes.

"Be glad I don't fire you," she said.

Fast-forward about five years, to middle school, which is the age when you first realize it's not fun if some kids have the latest cool thing and you don't.

It was the first day back, after summer vacation. Which is a really weird day, as we all know. Everyone was busy checking each other out, like, "What were you up to?" "Did you have a better summer than me? That would really make me mad if you did."

Even the teachers were checking each other out, mostly for new hairstyles. (Which I don't support, by the way. I think teachers should always have to look the same forever.)

Anyway, like I said it was the first day back, and our story begins pretty much where everything in life begins: the school cafeteria.

We were smack in the middle of lunch, and, as usual, Eliza Collins was the center of attention. (It's not just that she was really pretty, but she was also really rich. In other words, she was really lucky. She must have been like a saint or a seeing-eye dog in a former life.)

She was showing everyone her amazingly amazing new

device: a battery-operated robot that looked like a one-foot-tall tiny metal person.

"It's called the Botman," Eliza announced, as the little guy walked around in circles, making a loud beeping sound.

A bunch of us gathered around, trying to decide if we were awed, annoyed, or both. "And check this out—this is the coolest part."

She pushed a button, and Botman said, "Yo, Eliza, it's Wednesday! That means tennis lesson at four, manicure at five-thirty." Everybody *ooh*-ed and *aah*-ed, including me.

She pushed another button, and Botman said, "Yo, Eliza, dress light today! Forecast calls for mild temps, with a high of eighty-two degrees."

Everybody *wow*-ed and *cool*-ed, including me.

Then Eliza picked up her chocolate milk carton and placed it in Botman's outstretched little arms, and he motored over to the garbage can and threw it in—swish.

"Thank you, Botman," said Eliza.

"No problem, yo," replied Botman.

The crowd went crazy, and that was the exact moment I decided I had to have one.

Eliza was just about to push another button on Botman

when a voice suddenly rang out from the back of the crowd.

"We get it."

Everyone turned around. There was Katie Friedman, rolling her eyes at no one in particular.

This was nothing unusual, of course. Katie's a professional eye-roller. It's one of the things I love most about her.

"You get what?" Eliza demanded.

We all waited.

"We get that you're always the first person with a cool new gadget thingie that most of the rest of us will never even get to touch, much less own," Katie said. That pretty much summed up what everyone was feeling, even though we were all too busy being impressed to even realize it.

Then she added, "Yo."

The crowd roared happily; nobody minded the richest and prettiest girl in the grade getting embarrassed every once in a while. Eliza blushed, the bell rang, and we headed to our next class. I looked at Katie and remembered an important lesson: It didn't matter how rich you were, there were some things that money couldn't buy.

And hearing a bunch of kids laugh at something you said was totally priceless.

"That Botman thingie is pretty cool," I said to my friend Timmy McGibney, as we filed into Spanish.

"Yeah," Timmy said, not looking me in the eye.

I immediately got suspicious.

Timmy and I have had our ups and downs. We've been friends for so long that sometimes it felt more like we were brothers, which meant that we fought and got mad at each other and got on each other's nerves just as much as real brothers did.

And, like typical brothers, we could get pretty jealous of each other's stuff.

Plus, I knew his birthday was coming up.

"You're not getting the Botman, are you?" I asked.

Timmy looked at me and smiled. "Maybe."

I was just about to bombard him with questions when a sharp clapping sound changed the subject.

"Ya basta!" shouted our Spanish teacher, Señora Glickstein. (The other Spanish teacher was named Señor O'Brien. Go figure.)

"We'll talk about this later," I whispered to Timmy, as

we opened our books and tried to care about the differ-
ence between *ser* and *estar*.

If good parenting means not spoiling your kids and not buying them a lot of things, then my parents are the best parents in the world.

Which is fine; I'm not one of these kids who cares about having things like pool tables and Ping-Pong tables and go-carts and refrigerators full of soda and an arcade in my basement with tons of different video game systems.

As long as my friends have them, and I can use theirs.

That day after school, I was at my friend Jake Katz's house, and we were jumping on his trampoline—another thing I don't have—and talking about the Botman.

"Katie's takedown of Eliza was awesome," Jake said, while alternating landings on his feet and his butt.

"Yeah," I said, "but the Botman was pretty cool."

Jake made a face. "Ugh. Another gadget. Enough already."

"What do you mean?" I asked. Jake was considered one of the smartest kids in the school, and I figured it was always good to know where he stood on things.

He thought for a second. (It was hard to look thoughtful while jumping up and down, but somehow Jake pulled it off.)

"I just think this whole technological revolution thing has gotten out of control," Jake said, somehow managing to prevent his glasses from flying off his head. "We've become slaves to our devices. You should see my mom. She texts me twenty times a day. And the minute my dad gets home from work, he's on his cell phone or his computer all night, reading the news or staring at his e-mails. When we ask him a question, it takes him ten minutes just to hear it."

It was true. Jake's dad was definitely one of those workaholic, distracted genius types who didn't say much. My theory had always been that he was just tuning out Jake's mom, because she talks nonstop.

But maybe Jake was right. Maybe the world had become too dependent on technology.

I continued to bounce, thinking about what Jake said, and then I thought about Timmy's birthday again. Suddenly I had this vision of Eliza and Timmy comparing Botmans in the school cafeteria, while I sat there staring at my soggy fish sticks.

Which is when I realized that I wanted to be just as dependent on technology as everybody else.

"Let's go jump in the pool," I said, hoping a change of scenery would do me good.

"Okay," Jake said, agreeable as always.

As we jumped in, I decided that it was easy for Jake to be all high and mighty about how we've all become slaves to our possessions. He was the one with a trampoline and a pool.

I was mad at him for a split second. But then my body hit the perfectly heated, eighty-degree water, and I realized that pools and jealousy don't mix.

5

I brought up the idea of getting a Botman at dinner that night.

"I think it will help me do better in school," was my argument. (What? You wanted me to go with "Whatever the other kids have, I want"?)

My dad laughed. "How so?" he asked. "Will it invent excuses for why you didn't do your homework? Will it actually read the books for you?"

I have a bit of an issue with reading, in case you haven't heard. Not a big fan.

"It will help me get organized," I insisted. "It will tell me what assignments I have to do, and what tests I have coming up, and remind me to study, stuff like that."

My mom is a kind, patient person who always tries to give me the benefit of the doubt, but this was a stretch, even for her. She smiled, but shook her head. "You already have a cell phone, Charlie Joe. We just can't justify buying you an expensive new thingamajig right now."

I wanted to say, *But Eliza has one, and Timmy is about to get one!* But that didn't seem like an argument I could win. So instead I said, "Soon everybody will have one except me," which I have to admit sounded a little lame.

15

Dad shook his head. "Just the fact that you have a cell phone at your age is hard to take. In my day you were lucky if you were allowed to use the phone at all." Dad was a big in-my-day guy. If you believed everything he said about how hard things were in his day, you would be amazed that he lived long enough to tell us about it.

"Fine," I mumbled, admitting defeat. And then, right on cue, my phone buzzed.

From Timmy.

`Guess what I got?`

There was only one response to that, which I typed immediately.

`Chicken pox?`

I waited. My phone buzzed. I read the text.

`I'll give you a hint—It rhymes with shmotman.`

Charlie Joe's Financial Tip #1

NEVER DO SOMETHING YOURSELF IF YOU CAN GET SOMEONE ELSE TO DO IT.

Americans take great pride in getting someone else to do their work for them, and it's a sign you've made it to the top when you're able to do it. Whether it's a factory boss, an army general, or a football coach, everyone knows that the best way to get ahead is to figure out how to get everyone else to work while you sit back and get the glory.

I believe deeply in that philosophy, and I follow it every chance I get.

In fact, I'm following it with this book, which is why Katie Friedman is going to write the next chapter.

I'll be playing with the dogs, if anyone needs me.

Hi, my name is Katie Friedman.

My friend Charlie Joe Jackson asked me to write a chapter for his new book and, since I wasn't doing anything else particularly fascinating today, I said sure.

Charlie Joe said he wanted me to do it because he thought a female perspective would be interesting and that he values my insights and keenly intelligent mind.

Give me a break. He's not fooling anybody.

You and I both know there's only one reason he asked me to write a chapter for his book.

He's the laziest person on earth.

But even though he's lazy, and even though he's obnoxious, and even though he drives me crazy on a regular basis, I still find myself wanting to make him happy.

It's trying to figure out weird things like that that make me want to become a therapist someday.

♥ ♥ ♥

So I was just finishing a rehearsal with my band CHICKMATE (kind of an emo-rock-blues thing) when Charlie Joe texted me all in a panic, because Eliza had a

Botman, and Timmy just got a Botman, too, and Charlie Joe's parents refused to buy him one.

If you want to talk to me, call me, I texted back. I'm kind of over texts. Texts are like those notes you pass back and forth to each other in second grade when the teacher's not looking. I mean, come on people, grow up.

Anyway, two seconds later my phone rang. Guess who?

"See, Charlie Joe?" I said. "I don't have a fancy-schmancy little robot helper, but when you call me, I still somehow manage to answer the phone! It's a miracle!"

"I'm not in the mood," Charlie Joe answered. "I need your advice."

"My advice comes laced with comedy," I said, which made my bandmates laugh.

"Where are you?" he asked.

"Just had rehearsal. You're coming to Jake's bar mitzvah on Friday, right?"

(It's true, Jake actually hired us to play at his bar mitzvah! Well, technically his dad hired us, probably because he went to college with my dad. Anyway, it was going to be our first ever gig, and I was thrilled! And petrified.)

"We'll see," Charlie Joe said, even though he was obviously going, since Jake is one of his best friends.

"Well, you better think we're awesome, or I'll never give you advice again," I said, and I meant it. Don't mess with me and my music.

"Fine." Then Charlie Joe sighed into the phone, which meant we were through talking about something other than him. "I need a job," he said.

Now, you have to have known this kid for as long as I have to truly appreciate the hilarious nature of that statement.

"I'm sorry, who are you and what have you done with Charlie Joe Jackson?"

"I'm serious. I need to find a job where I can make some money."

Slowly, the momentousness of the occasion began to dawn on me. The most infamous slacker in our entire middle school, the kid who would rather write a book than read a book, the kid who would rather dress up in a ridiculous costume than pay attention in class . . . that kid actually wants a JOB?!

I whistled into the phone. "Meet me downtown in twenty minutes."

♥ ♥ ♥

Twenty-two minutes later, we were sitting on a bench outside Jookie's, which is the local youth club where kids go to pretend that parents don't exist. Sometimes Jookie's has concerts where high school bands play, so I took a quick look inside and imagined myself up on that stage, singing one of my original songs (even though I haven't actually written one yet), with the crowd waving their arms in the air, chanting, "CHICKMATE! CHICK-MATE! CHICKMATE!"

Oh, wait, sorry. This is Charlie Joe's book, not mine, right?

Anyway, we're sitting there, and Charlie Joe looked sadder than a dog who's just finished his dinner. Which is an appropriate metaphor, since he brought along his two big lab mixes, Moose and Coco. They were pulling on their leashes so enthusiastically it looked like they were going to yank Charlie Joe's arms right out of their sockets.

"Do these guys go everywhere with you?" I asked.

"Everywhere they're allowed," Charlie Joe said, "and some places they're not."

"So tell me, exactly what line of work are you looking to get into?" I tried to imagine Charlie Joe in a work environment. It wasn't easy.

"It's not work I'm looking for," he answered. "It's money."

I stared at him. "Really? I had no idea. That is truly shocking."

Suddenly, Charlie Joe went flying, courtesy of Moose and Coco, who had spotted a squirrel and decided to give chase. The squirrel got away, but the dogs didn't seem to mind.

I ran up to the dogs and petted their awesomely soft coats. "Have they ever caught one?"

"Nah," Charlie Joe said. "But they never lose hope. I don't think they remember that their batting average is zero." He scratched their ears. "Isn't that right, you big dummies?"

Moose answered by jumping up and swiping his enormous tongue across Charlie Joe's face. Charlie Joe then proceeded to lie down on the ground and act like a dog for five minutes, while the actual dogs jumped on, over, and around him. In public! It was adorable and ridiculous at the same time.

"I didn't come down here to watch you do your best Scooby-Doo imitation," I said.

All three of them looked up at me, panting.

"Sorry," said Charlie Joe. "Where were we? Oh, yeah. I need money. I really want a Botman, and my parents won't buy it for me. So I'm looking for a job where I can make a lot of money pretty fast, like two hundred bucks, but won't be hard or take a lot of work."

Isn't he adorable?

"I'll put my best people on it," I said. Then the four of us walked down to the river, where the dogs chased some ducks. Ducks can fly, though, and dogs can't, so it wasn't exactly a fair fight.

We were sitting by the river, watching the dogs wish they could fly, when the idea suddenly hit me.

"I've got it," I said to Charlie Joe.

"You've got what?"

"A way you can make money that you might actually enjoy."

Charlie Joe jumped up. "I could kiss you!"

"I don't think Nareem would appreciate that," I said quickly. Nareem Ramdal is my boyfriend, BTW. He's awesome.

"Duh. I was kidding," Charlie Joe said.

"Oh. Right."

Charlie Joe sat back down. "Now, tell me how I'm gonna get rich," he said.

So I told him.

♥ ♥ ♥

Okay, I'm going to give you back to Charlie Joe now.

Ladies and gentlemen, how about a hand for Katie Friedman?

I thought she did an awesome job. If I could, I would definitely have Katie write the rest of this book. But I can't have someone calling me "the laziest person on earth" in public, even if it's true.

She described what happened pretty accurately, though. I did call her in a panic, because she always seems to be the best person to talk to on those incredibly rare occasions when I can't figure something out myself.

And it's true, we were by the river watching the dogs wish they could fly, when suddenly she smiled that Katie smile—the one that meant all my problems were solved—and said to me, "I've got it."

Then she told me her plan, and I got incredibly excited. It sounded perfect. It was Katie's idea. And as we all know, Katie's never wrong, right?

Wrong.

The next day at school, I put the plan into action. The first thing I did was made sure to participate a lot in my English class. I make a point of participating in all my classes—because I find it can get you out of doing actual work—but this was different, because my guidance counselor, Ms. Ferrell, was observing class that day, and I wanted to make sure she noticed. And she did. After answering yet another question correctly, Ms. Ferrell said, "I have to say, Charlie Joe, you are really on your game today."

So far, so good.

At the end of class, while the rest of the kids got out of there as fast as their little legs would take them, I casually followed Ms. Ferrell back to her office. When she saw me coming, she smiled and shook her head.

"Uh-oh," she said.

I laughed and glanced out into the hall, where Timmy was keeping an eye on me. He'd been showing kids his new Botman all morning, but I'd been ignoring him—just to annoy him, of course. Now he was trying to decide whether it was worth being late to his next class in order to wait for me and rub his new toy in my face. I chased him away, because I had business to attend to.

I picked up the picture of Misty, Ms. Ferrell's beloved pet Great Dane, which she kept on her desk.

"That is one beautiful dog," I said.

Ms. Ferrell looked over my shoulder and nodded in agreement. "There's nothing I wouldn't do for that girl. And I have the medical bills to prove it."

"Well, it's funny you say that, because I had this idea," I say, perfectly innocently. "You know how you're always talking about how you wish Misty could get more exercise?"

Ms. Ferrell eyed me suspiciously. "Actually, I'm *not* always talking about that," she said, "but go on."

"Well, I've heard you say how because of your schedule and driving your kids around after school you never get to take her out enough," I said, mentally crossing my fingers.

Ms. Ferrell picked up the picture of her dog and started petting it. (I love Ms. Ferrell, but she had a few strange habits, and this was one of them.)

"What are you getting at, Charlie Joe?"

I took a deep breath. "Well, I've decided to start a dog-walking business, and I was thinking that maybe I could walk Misty after school for you. I'm great with dogs, they really listen to me, and I'm going to find some other dogs to walk so they can all play with each other. It's going to be amazing. They'll love it."

"How much?" Ms. Ferrell asked.

Wow, she really knew how to get down to business.

Unfortunately, I didn't. "Well, in terms of payment, I was thinking, um, whatever you think is fair . . ." I continued to stammer along like that for a minute or so before she cut me off.

"I mean, how much extra credit are you hoping to get with this project? Is this another way for you to try and get your grades up? Do you think this will make me care less about your spotty behavior and your reading habits and you fulfilling your potential?"

She laughed softly, and I knew I had my first customer.

"I would never think that," I said, but I'm pretty sure she wasn't convinced.

After I sold Ms. Ferrell on the idea, it was easy to sign up her friends Ms. Rathbone (bulldog named Buster), Mr. Dormer (dachshund named Schleppy), and Ms. Costello (mixed breed rescue dog named Atom— Ms. C was a science teacher). I had it all figured out, thanks to Katie. My mom would drive me to their houses three times a week after school to pick up their dogs and take them to the park for two hours, where they could all play. I would get paid six dollars per dog. Which added up to twenty-four dollars a day. Which added up to seventy-two dollars a week. Which added up to a brand-new Botman in about four weeks.

Which added up to a very happy Charlie Joe.

When I told the guys the plan at lunch, most of them were pretty impressed. Pete Milano smacked me hard on the back—he didn't mean anything by it, that's just how he is—and told me I should take dog poop and put it on Vice Principal Farber's doorstep, which was a really stupid idea, considering Vice Principal Farber lived two houses down from me.

Nareem Ramdal—who was Katie's boyfriend and who had become a good friend of mine over the summer at

Camp Rituhbukkee—congratulated me on my "first foray into the world of capitalism." Nareem uses at least one word I've never heard of in every sentence.

Timmy's reaction was a little more complicated. His first instinct was to try to poke holes in the whole plan.

"You're getting paid just to play with a bunch of dogs?!"

"Yup."

He looked like he was about to choke on his fish stick. "What happens if one of the dogs doesn't want to go with you?" he asked.

"Dogs love me," I answered. Which is true; dogs do love me. You know that phrase *man's best friend*? Well, I'm that man.

Timmy thought about that for a minute, then immediately changed his mind and decided he wanted to become my partner. "Well, are you sure you can handle four dogs by yourself? What if one of them runs away or something? I could totally help you."

I looked at him. "For free?"

"I'm sure we can come to some sort of arrangement," he said, which sounded like a phrase he must have heard on some lawyer TV show.

Right at that moment Hannah Spivero walked up, and all conversation stopped.

Then she sat down at the table, and all movement of any kind stopped.

You may have heard that in my humble opinion, Hannah

Spivero is the closest thing to perfection in human form. Timmy kind of feels the same way. Most of the other boys in our grade (wrongly) think she comes in somewhere behind Eliza Collins, but she's still important enough for all activity to come to a grinding halt when she shows up unannounced.

"Have you guys seen Jake?"

Oh, right. Jake Katz. Her boyfriend. You know the type of guy who's great at sports, really good-looking, effortlessly charming with the ladies, got it all going on? Well, Jake's the opposite. And Hannah loves him for it. Go figure.

I appreciated any opportunity to talk to Hannah, though—even if it was to help her find her boyfriend-that-wasn't-me—so I answered before anyone else could.

"No," I said helpfully.

Awesomely, Hannah didn't immediately get up and go look for him. "Were you guys talking about dogs?" she asked. She was staring straight at me, which had its typical effect of turning my face into the surface of the sun.

"Charlie Joe is starting a dog-walking business," Timmy said, butting in as usual. "He's already got four dogs lined up from teachers."

"Actually, I prefer to call it a canine recreation program," I said, trying to sound clever.

"Cool," Hannah said. "I love dogs."

I was all set to describe my intense love for dogs—which probably would have led to her realizing how much we had in common, which probably would have led to me saying that from the moment I laid eyes on her I knew we were destined to be together, which probably would have led to her saying you are so right, why have I been wasting time with Jake when I could have been with you all along, which probably would have led to us climbing over the lunch table, knocking trays of half-eaten cheeseburgers and half-drunk chocolate milks all over the floor in order to stare into each other's eyes, and possibly even kiss—but she got up before I got the chance.

"Maybe Jake's in the library," she said, walking away. "Good luck with the dog thing."

Okay, so no big love scene with Hannah today. Moving on.

"When's Jake's bar mitzvah?" huge Phil Manning asked, changing the subject. His girlfriend, tiny Celia Barbarossa, giggled. They were the most mature, serious couple in the grade, and they loved bar mitzvahs, because it meant plenty of time for kissing, which had recently replaced football (Phil) and violin (Celia) as their favorite activity.

I shrugged. "Friday, I think." There was at least one bar mitzvah, confirmation, or birthday party every weekend, and they all blended together into one long, endless parade of souvenir sweatshirts, dance wranglers, chocolate fountains, bus rides, photo booths, slide shows, and checks that my parents got a little sick of writing. ("Do I even know this kid?" was what my dad usually said.) Jake's bar mitzvah was going to be a doozy, at some country club turned into an indoor baseball field, with a buffet set up in the infield and a dance floor in the outfield. Rumors were flying that two actual New York Yankees were going to be signing autographs. And Phil and Celia would probably be kissing in the right field bleachers.

"So do you want me to help you with the dogs or not?" Timmy said, changing the subject back.

I looked at him skeptically. "Since when do you like dogs?"

"Since now," he said, scarfing down the last of his ice cream sandwich.

Charlie Joe's Financial Tip #2

YOU CAN GET MONEY WITHOUT WORKING.

There are lots of ways to make sure you're getting paid, and none of them involve working. Here's a short list of a few ways to keep the cash coming:

1. *Call your grandparents on their birth-days—they'll send you a check on yours.*
2. *Get $3.00 for lunch money. Then pay some kid $1.00 to split his lunch and keep $2.00. Everybody wins.*
3. *Collect all the loose change around the house and put it in a big bottle. Say it's the "family fund." It's not. It's the "you fund."*
4. *Babysit for kids who love television as much as you do.*
5. *Open a lemonade stand—but only after your mom makes the lemonade and your dad makes the stand.*

It turned out my mom had a doctor's appointment, so my sister's boyfriend Willy drove me and Timmy to pick up the dogs on my first day of work.

My first day of work! Holy moly, that sounds so awesome. Hello, money. Hello, Botman.

"So what are you going to do with the cash?" Willy asked.

"I'm going to buy a Botman," I answered.

"I already have a Botman," Timmy said unnecessarily.

Willy looked at him. "So then why are you here?"

"I just like money," Timmy explained.

I decided to let Timmy join my dog-walking business for three reasons: 1) he was happy with eight dollars a day, leaving me the other sixteen; 2) he was as fascinated by Hannah Spivero as I was, so I figured we'd have plenty to talk about on the job; and 3) holding four dogs on four leashes at the same time seemed a little impossible.

"Well, just be careful with those dogs," Willy said, as we turned into Ms. Rathbone's driveway. "I'm sure they're incredibly cute, but they're still animals, with animal instincts and animal needs and animal urges."

Timmy and I looked at each other.

"What's your point?" I asked Willy.

He laughed. "They don't call it a dog-eat-dog world for nothing," he said, as Buster the bulldog sprinted down the driveway and crash-landed into the back seat at full speed.

* * *

After we picked up all the dogs—although Atom refused to get in until we threw a piece of beef jerky inside—we headed to Lake Monahan. Willy's pickup truck was filled to the brim—since we'd also taken Moose and Coco, we had six dogs crammed in there, or seven, if you count Misty the Great Dane as two dogs, which you should. But they all seemed thrilled to be out and about, riding in the back of a truck, their ears pinned back by the wind as they smacked each other in the head with their tails. Schleppy, the dachshund, was a total munchkin compared to the other dogs—in fact, he probably could have easily fit inside one of Misty's ears—but he was clearly the

leader of the pack. When he barked, people (and dogs) listened.

At the lake, Willy dropped us off and drove away, chuckling and shaking his head.

Timmy and I looked around. Now that we were out there with the dogs, we didn't quite know what to do.

"Let's head to the Rock," Timmy said.

Lake Monahan is a beautiful place, with a big field to play in and a lake for the dogs to cool off in when they get hot. The Rock is the watering hole where all the dogs gather and make friends. It's the butt-sniffing capital of the world.

Moose and Coco didn't need leashes, but we were under strict orders never to let the other dogs off theirs. So once we got to the Rock, our first problem was to figure out how to let the dogs go swimming.

"I have an idea," Timmy said, as Misty was introducing himself to a friendly golden retriever named Sonny. "We just have to make sure the dogs are on their leashes, right? Nobody said that we had to be holding their leashes the whole time."

I considered his point. Technically, he was right. As long as the dogs were "on" their leashes, it was all good.

We dropped the leashes and the dogs made a mad dash to the water, except for Schleppy, who was more interested in taking a snooze; he parked himself under a picnic table. There had to have been at least twenty dogs there, splashing and chasing sticks and dog-paddling, and they were clearly having a blast. Timmy and I took a seat to watch the festivities.

"Sure beats working for a living," I said.

"This it too good to be true," Timmy said.

Turned out we were both right.

11

The dogs had been swimming for about fifteen minutes—and Timmy and I had been talking about Hannah Spivero for about fourteen of those minutes—when we heard a voice behind us.

"How's the whole dog-walking thing going?"

Guess who?

We turned around and there was Hannah, holding a leash with a gigantic poodle at the end of it.

Jake was there, too. He wasn't on a leash.

"What are you guys doing here?" I asked, while noticing out of the corner of my eye that Buster was trying to get inappropriately friendly with a springer spaniel. "Buster!" I hollered, and he turned and gave me a look as if to say, *Stop interrupting.*

"I always take Gladys for a walk here after school," Hannah said.

"Which one's Gladys?" I asked, looking back and forth between Jake and the poodle.

"Ha-ha," Jake said, looking at me suspiciously. Even though Jake and I were good friends, he was always on the lookout for any signs that I might be moving in on his girl, which was flattering, since Hannah was about as interested in me as a vegetarian is in a pork chop.

"What were you two talking about?" Hannah asked Timmy and me, as if she didn't know.

"I can't remember," I answered.

As if on cue, Misty came over and shook herself off, flinging a disgusting mixture of mud, drool, and lake water all over my clothes.

"Gross!" Timmy seemed to say, although I couldn't quite tell, since he was laughing so hard.

I looked at Buster and Atom, who were still in the water, pretending to swim but really just scoping out the girl dogs. I realized I hadn't brought any towels, and thought about how thrilled my mom was going to be when she picked us up and discovered her car was about to be ruined forever.

Hannah's dog, meanwhile, seemed perfectly content to remain on the shore, obviously too considerate to ruin Hannah's typically perfect outfit.

"This dog thing seems like it's the perfect job for you," Jake said.

"Thanks," I responded, even though I was pretty sure he didn't mean it as a compliment.

"You get to sit under a tree and talk about my girl-friend, and get paid for it," Jake continued, confirming my suspicions.

"Well, it's a lot of responsibility," Timmy jumped in,

"and talking about Hannah just makes the time go faster."
He had a habit of trying to come to my rescue and instead
making things worse.

"I'm glad I could help," Hannah said, trying to make
everyone happy, but actually just making everyone uncomfortable. Then, realizing she should probably change
the subject, Hannah looked around and added, "I thought
you guys said you were babysitting four dogs."

"We are," I said.

"Then where's the fourth dog?"

I felt a weird burning sensation in the pit of my stomach. I jumped up and started walking toward the picnic
table. After a second, my walking turned into jogging, and
then into sprinting.

I reached the table, said a tiny little prayer to myself,
then got down on my knees and looked underneath.

No Schleppy.

Oh, no.

I immediately started to panic.

"Where's Schleppy?" Timmy yelled, which only suc-
ceeded in making every other dog owner turn and look
at me. Somehow they managed to look worried and accu-
satory at the same time.

"I don't know," I said, seeing my life flash before my eyes.

I had lost an eighteen-pound dog in a thousand-acre
forest.

Of all the horrible thoughts that raced through my mind at that very moment, one kept fighting its way to the front:

I was pretty sure the whole Botman thing was never going to happen.

The first thing I had to do was wade into the muddy lake and gather up Buster and Atom. They weren't too happy about leaving their new friends, but the freaked-out quality in my voice got their attention, and they hustled out of the water. Misty was on the shore, alert, ready to roll. Moose and Coco were sniffing around the nearby bushes. It was almost as if all the dogs knew exactly what was going on and were already looking for Schleppy.

I felt like I had my own little canine police force, which made me feel a little better. Not a lot. A little.

Jake and Hannah were ahead of us, calling to Schleppy. Timmy and I spread out, each with a couple of dogs, examining every inch of that place. Holy moly, it never felt so big.

After a while I glanced at my watch. My mom was due to pick us up in fifteen minutes. Not a lot of time to find a tiny dog with an appetite for adventure.

"Find Schleppy! Find Schleppy!" I urged the dogs as we ran through the park, hoping their sixth sense would help them understand exactly what I was saying. It seemed like they did, except for the times where they would suddenly decide to chase a squirrel or a duck and my arms would come out of my sockets.

I'd been sprinting at top speed—well, my top speed—for about five minutes when I suddenly noticed a different feeling in my stomach. I'd gone from panic to nausea. I'm not going to lie, I'm not in the best shape in the world, and this was way more exercise than my body was used to.

Timmy texted me:

Any luck?

I texted back:

Not yet.

He texted back:

Me neither.

Schleppy was lost. And I was losing hope.

Then, a gift from heaven. Hannah texted me:

Jake has an idea.

When the smartest kid in the grade has an idea, you listen. I texted back:

Yeah?

I waited eight long seconds. Then I got the text:

We're heading to the mill.

The Mill was a part of Lake Monahan that I almost never went to, because it didn't have any water for Moose and Coco to play in. Plus you had to go up one huge hill, then down another, then up another—just to get to an open field, where there were tons of small holes in the ground that you could easily break an ankle in, if you weren't careful. Supposedly there had been a big mill there once, although I didn't even really know what a mill was and certainly didn't care. But apparently all the holes were from giant machines that had been uprooted from the ground.

It shocked me to think that a tiny dog could make it all the way to the Mill, considering I barely could. But it was worth a try, so off we went.

It was far. If the dogs weren't there to pull me along then I'm not sure I would have made it.

But I had a job to do, and I was determined to do it. Plus, I definitely was going to be grounded for life if this didn't end well.

I met up with Timmy, and we headed up the first hill, which now that I was actually on it, definitely felt more like a mountain. Timmy was an excellent skateboarder and lacrosse player, and he wasn't huffing and puffing at all. I was an excellent Xbox player, and I was about to collapse.

Then we went down the next hill. The dogs picked up speed, and I almost fell five times. It felt like one of those movies where all the huskies are running through the snow carrying a huge sled, only instead of yelling, "MUSH!" I was yelling, "SLOW DOWN OR I'M GONNA BREAK MY FREAKIN' NECK!"

In case you were wondering, people were watching us with shocked looks on their faces.

We finally made it up the last hill and got to the Mill.

There they were, those weird little holes, and sure enough, I almost broke my ankle in the very first one. I suddenly wondered why anyone would come here willingly, unless they had a thing for crutches.

I saw Hannah and Jake waving frantically, and we sprinted over to them, side-stepping the holes as best as we could.

Jake pointed, and I stopped in my tracks. So did all the dogs. I looked down, and I saw what looked like the back half of Schleppy's body sticking out of a hole.

Half-Schleppy's tail was wagging happily. In a minute, so was mine.

"SCHLEPPY!" I yelled, and the dog emerged from his hole, face covered in dirt and grass. He looked at me casually, as if he hadn't caused me a heart attack.

Then he plunged his face right back in the hole.

All the other dogs wanted in on Schleppy's action. As

they fought over snout space—they needed to know what was down that one hole, and didn't seem to care that there were a thousand other holes just like it—I turned to Jake and Hannah.

"You guys saved my life," I said, without exaggeration. "What happened? Why did you look here? How did you know?"

Jake looked at the ground, which is what he always does when he's about to say something that makes people remember he's smarter than everyone else. "Dachshunds were bred to hunt and chase burrow-dwelling animals," he informed us. "When Hannah told me about this part of the park that had a lot of burrowlike holes, I figured that might be where he would go."

Then Hannah gave Jake a "my boyfriend's a genius" kiss, and even though Jake was still looking at the ground I could tell he was smiling.

I felt a pang of jealousy, but then realized that only a selfish jerk would be jealous of someone who had just completely saved his life. So I fist-bumped him and said, "Thank you so much, dude. You are the MAN."

Even though I was still jealous, that at least makes me a little less of a jerk, right?

13

We were still celebrating our successful search-and-rescue mission when Misty saw something move out of the corner of her eye and decided to plunge full-speed ahead into the nearby bushes.

Have you ever held the leash of a full-speed-ahead lunging Great Dane?

Neither had I.

Misty dragged me for about ten feet before I decided to preserve whatever muscles I still had in my left arm and let go of the leash. She launched herself into the bushes and you could feel the earth move, kind of like that scene in *Jurassic Park* when the Tyrannosaurus Rex first makes his entrance.

That was followed by an enormous amount of thrashing, crashing, and howling. All the humans and dogs turned their heads toward the ruckus. Moose and Coco started barking wildly. Buster the bulldog paced back and forth, trying to breathe through his nose. Atom was jumping up and down, which isn't easy to do when you're on a leash.

Even Schleppy emerged from her precious hole to see what was going on.

Suddenly the noise and the thrashing stopped. There was a brief moment when I thought everything was going to be fine, Misty would come out of the bushes and we could just go home, and I could return all the dogs to their rightful owners and tell them what a great time I had with their dogs, but had decided I had too much studying to do and was therefore resigning from the dog-sitting business.

Misty finally re-emerged, wagging her tail proudly. All would have been well, except for one small problem.

She had a gopher in her mouth.

That's right. A *gopher.*

The poor little guy was very much alive, and seemed totally calm, like he had already decided he was going to a better place and was ready to accept his fate.

Moose and Coco looked on, awestruck. They'd never caught anything in their lives.

"Drop it!" I ordered Misty.

She laughed at me with her eyes.

After a few more lame attempts at getting Misty to

release the animal, I did the only thing I could think of. I begged Jake to save me, again.

"Help me, Jake. What should I do?"

"I have no idea," Jake answered.

So the good news was, at last I knew what it took to stump Jake—a gopher thinking about heaven while stuck in a Great Dane's jaws. I was able to take some comfort in the fact that Jake was as clueless as me, but it was a tiny blip that was quickly overwhelmed by a huge blob of panic.

"Misty, drop it," I ordered again. She didn't.

"Misty, drop it NOW," I insisted.

Oh, please, she might as well have answered.

Timmy was standing there, doing something that looked suspiciously like giggling. I stared at him, and he kicked a pebble.

Hannah was texting someone. Probably the whole grade. And it probably said:

`Omg Charlie Joe is so getting de-`
`tention.`

Finally Jake said, "Charlie Joe, what are you going to do?"

Everyone waited for me to make the next move. I guess this is what it was like being the boss. I guess this is why I make the big bucks.

Suddenly I wanted to be the guy who made the little bucks.

Misty decided she wanted to carry the poor gopher all the way home.

The interesting thing was, she didn't really seem to have any desire to kill it, or eat it, or even harm it in any way.

I think she wanted to keep it as a pet.

Once we let Hannah and Jake get back to their previously scheduled romantic walk in the park, Timmy and I started the long trek back to the parking lot. But by the time we managed to coax Schleppy from his hole, gather up the other overstimulated dogs, fight with them when they wanted to swim in every watering hole on the way out of the park, and stop for the one guy who thought he could pry the gopher from Misty's jaws, only to find out the hard way that Misty really didn't like people trying to take things from her, we were twenty minutes late.

My mom was standing outside her car with an unthrilled look on her face. Timmy's mom was standing outside her car, too, because we needed two cars to take us all home.

Which meant twice as much explaining.

When she saw Misty and her new friend, the first thing

my mom did was get back in the car, shut the door, and take out her phone. Five seconds later I got a text.

I don't want to yell and scare the animals, but let me be perfectly clear: that thing's not getting in my car.

Mrs. McGibney, who was the nicest woman in the world besides my mom, came over to see what was going on. When she saw the gopher she put her hands to her chest and exclaimed, "Oh, my word!"

I opened the back door to my mom's car to throw in the leashes and let Moose and Coco jump in through the hatchback. Meanwhile, Buster, Atom, Schleppy, and Timmy got in Mrs. McGibney's car.

That left me, Misty, and Mr. Gopher on the outside looking in.

Then—for some reason known only to her—Misty picked that very moment to finally set the gopher free.

The gopher made a beeline for the quickest shelter it could find, which happened to be in the backseat of our car. It jumped in before I could react.

My mom screamed. Moose and Coco, who were behind the fence in the back of the car, could not believe they were so close to a very catchable animal, and yet so far. They decided to show their frustration by barking as loud as they'd ever barked in their lives.

Mr. Gopher quickly realized he'd picked a bad spot, so

he darted out of the car and started sprinting through the parking lot.

Misty quickly realized she missed having Mr. Gopher as a pet and started sprinting after him.

I quickly realized that I didn't want to be a dog-sitter anymore.

Cars started weaving to avoid the dog, and one actually veered into the picnic area. People were yelling and screaming, "Catch your freakin' dog!" as if I were intentionally staying twenty-five feet behind it.

Finally Mr. Gopher ducked under a fence to freedom!

I'm pretty sure I saw him high-fiving two other gophers on the other side.

Misty peered under the same fence, quickly realized the fun was over, and came trotting back to me, wagging her tail, as if she were greeting an old friend.

I grabbed her leash, sat down, and we both panted harder than we had in our entire lives.

As Timmy's mom drove away, I saw Timmy waving and laughing in the passenger seat, and Buster, Atom, and Schleppy fighting over the windows in the back.

Then my mom drove over to me and Misty. She rolled down the window, leaned out, and smiled.

"How was work today, dear?"

By the time we pulled up to Ms. Ferrell's house, Misty was sleeping like a baby.

How adorable.

Ms. Ferrell had a big smile on her face when she answered the door. I was almost flattered until I realized it was because her beloved dog was home at last.

"How was it?" she asked. "Did she give you any trouble?"

"Oh, no," I said. "No trouble at all."

"Terrific!" Ms. Ferrell said, rubbing a little spot behind Misty's left ear that made the dog howl like a coyote getting a massage. "She's a little wet. Did you let her wade in the water?"

"Just for a minute."

Ms. Ferrell reached for her purse. Then, because she had already collected my pay from the other teachers, she handed me twenty-four dollars.

"Same time Wednesday?" she asked.

I looked at the money. It felt so good in my hands. It felt like happiness. It felt like freedom.

Then I remembered the sight of the picnic table with Schleppy not underneath it, and the sight of Misty chasing

Mr. Gopher through the parking lot, and the half an hour of craziness in between.

"Actually, Ms. Ferrell, I've kind of decided that it's not a great time to be dog-sitting right now," I said, trying to look her in the eye but failing. "I should probably concentrate on my schoolwork and stuff, so I don't fall behind."

Ms. Ferrell looked at me. I don't think she'd ever heard the words *concentrate* and *schoolwork* come out of my mouth in the same sentence before.

"It was a lot harder than you thought, huh," she said.

"Yeah."

"A little too hard?"

"I guess so," I said.

She smiled.

"Well, at some point, Charlie Joe, you're going to realize that a good day's work feels just as good as a good night's rest," Ms. Ferrell said, and she stepped outside and waved at my mother, who was waiting in the car.

"Is that from a fortune cookie?" I asked.

"Nope, it's from life," she answered.

Then she patted my cheek, went back inside, and shut the door.

When I got back to the car, my mom gave me a look.

"What?" I said.

"Did you tell her about the gopher?"

I hemmed for a second, hawed for another, and then said, "No."

"I don't blame you," she said.

I waited for her to ask me if I told Ms. Ferrell about losing Schleppy, but then I realized I hadn't even told my mom that part, so no worries there.

But she did have one other question. "How much money did you make?"

"Twenty-four dollars," I said proudly.

"Give me half."

Are you kidding me?

"I'm not kidding," she said, as if I had said, *Are you kidding me?* out loud.

I said the obvious thing. "Why?"

My mom sighed. "Because this car isn't going to clean itself, and whenever a nervous gopher urinates in my car, I generally try to get the smell out as quickly as possible. I'd like the trained professionals to do it." She held out her hand. "Hurry up, before I ask for all of it."

I glumly handed over twelve bucks. Then we drove away, and I closed my eyes, suddenly feeling completely exhausted.

"Working's not for me," I said, stating the obvious, just before I passed out.

Charlie Joe's Financial Tip #3

IF YOU HAVE TO WORK, MAKE SURE IT INVOLVES SOMETHING YOU REALLY LIKE.

I'm not an idiot. I know that eventually everyone has to get some kind of job. That's the way the world is. But that doesn't mean you have to hate it. There are lots of jobs out there that are awesome. Here are a few that I plan on checking out:

1. *Ice cream store scooper*
2. *Movie theater usher*
3. *Bakery cupcake taster*
4. *Video game designer*
5. *Carnival ride tester*
6. *Television show reviewer*
7. *Book editor (KIDDING! Just making sure you were still paying attention.)*

Part Two
THE SHIRT AND THE TIE

17

Hi, it's me again. Katie Friedman.

I'm writing another chapter because Charlie Joe said it was the least I could do after his canine catastrophe.

Whatever. It's kind of fun, so why not?

Anyway, he called me up right after it happened and said, "Your streak of never being wrong is officially over."

Before I could answer, he added, "And when you're wrong, you're really, really, REALLY wrong."

Then he told me the whole story, and I guess I was pretty wrong. But there was something about the way he blamed me for the whole thing that made any sympathy I might have felt for him disappear. So I listened, I tried not to laugh, I laughed anyway, tried not to laugh harder, laughed harder anyway, and then eventually I had to put the phone down because I was laughing so hard that tears were coming out of my eyes.

"Katie? Katie, are you there?"

I got myself together and picked up the phone. I was able to say, "Wow, Charlie Joe, that sounds like a total—" before I collapsed in a fit of giggles.

He hung up.

Now, we all know how fragile a boy's ego can be, so

instead of doing what I wanted to do, which was to let him stew and fret and realize he shouldn't blame other people for his own mistakes, I called him back and tried to play nice.

"Charlie Joe, I'm sorry I gave you bad advice. I said you should dog-sit because you love dogs and I thought it might be fun for you. I guess that was a bad idea."

He snorted. "A bad idea? That's the understatement of the century."

That's what I get for trying to play nice.

And when he tacked on, "You just might want to keep your ideas to yourself for the time being," my patience wore out completely.

"Listen, Charlie Joe," I said, "all I said was that you might want to consider dog-sitting as a business opportunity. I never said take six dogs to Lake Monahan. I never said let them off the leash so they can run wild all over the park and scare a poor defenseless animal half to death. And I definitely never said bring Timmy into the operation, so you can secretly try to get him to do all the work while you just sit around counting your money."

That last part might have been a little unfair, but I didn't care. I was on a roll.

"So the next time you need a little bit of advice," I went on, "there are plenty of people you can call. Call Pete. Call Nareem. Call Jake. Call Eliza. I'd say call Hannah, but since we both know you can't form an actual complete sentence whenever you're in her presence, that's probably not such a good idea."

I took a deep breath and waited. Silence.

"Charlie Joe?"

"I'm here. What do you have against Hannah? Are you jealous or something?"

Now, putting aside the fact that I hadn't said anything negative at all about Hannah—all my insults were aimed squarely at Charlie Joe—it just so happens that I think Hannah Spivero is a great person, and I wasn't jealous of her in the slightest.

"I'm not jealous of Hannah Spivero in the slightest," I said, "and besides, I have band rehearsal, so I have to go."

I immediately realized the second part of that sentence had nothing to do with the first. I hate it when that happens. It means I'm no longer in control of the conversation.

Charlie Joe laughed, a tiny little laugh, but just enough to let me know that he thought he won that particular round.

"Okay, fine," he said. "Based on recent results, you should probably stick to music anyway, instead of trying to become a professional advice-giver."

"Stick it, Charlie Joe," I said, and hung up the phone.

Sometimes it's good to go back to basics.

I think it says a lot about me that I'm willing to let Katie write chapters—in MY book—that make me look kind of like a jerk.

I just wanted to say that publicly.

We can get back to the story now.

19

At dinner after the doggie disaster, when my mom told my dad all about it, the first thing he did was ask if all the animals were okay.

Then, when he found out they were, he laughed for about eighteen minutes straight.

Then he stopped laughing, looked at me, and said, "This isn't funny."

It's not?

"Money doesn't just grow on trees, as they say," Dad went on. "You have to work for it, and working is serious stuff. You can't decide that just because you need money and like dogs, you can become a professional dog-walker."

"Dog-sitter," I corrected.

"Whatever. The point is a job is something you have to prepare for, and take extremely seriously." He pointed at his briefcase, which was sitting by the door. "You think I just decided one day I wanted to be a lawyer, and the next day I went in front of a judge trying cases?"

"If you love being a lawyer so much," I asked, "then why do you drop your briefcase the second you walk in the door, and change out of your suit like you're allergic to it or something?"

"Watch it," he said, but I could tell by his face that he thought I had a point. "I didn't say I loved being a lawyer. I said I take it seriously because it's my job. Working is hard, that's just a fact of life, and the sooner you realize that, the better."

Then he clapped his hands together, which meant he had an idea, usually one that I wouldn't like.

"Hey, you know what? You should come to work with me for a day. Then you could see what getting a paycheck actually means."

I laughed. "Yeah, well the thing is, I have this little thing called *school*, so sadly that's not going to work out."

"You don't have school this Friday," my mom pointed out unhelpfully. "It's teacher development day."

Now, usually I loved teacher development day, like all kids, but suddenly I realized how ridiculous it was. What was it that teachers were constantly developing anyway?

"Ugh," I said, while I tried to think of another excuse not to go.

"I'll give you twenty bucks," my dad offered. "Think of it as a one-day, paid internship."

Hmm. Twenty bucks. No gophers. It could be worse.

"Fine," I said. "Whatever."

My dad chuckled. "See? Money always has the last word." Not really, since he was still talking. "We'll take the train in, hang out at the office, grab some lunch—we'll have

66

a great time. And you'll see what it really means to be a working man."

"That sounds like a splendid idea," my mom said, which was weird, since she never used the word *splendid*.

"Sorry I'm gonna miss it," my sister, Megan, chimed in, finally joining the conversation.

Then she winked at me, which I didn't appreciate.

Charlie Joe's Financial Tip #4

THERE'S NO SUCH THING AS A FREE RIDE, UNLESS YOU KNOW SOMEBODY.

Isn't it awesome when your dad, or your friend's dad, or your friend's mom gets free tickets to a game, and they want to take YOU? It's awesome because you know that if the tickets are free, then the seats are great. Because free things are always the best.

That's why it's so important to know someone who has access to free things.

The thing is, you can go through life one of two ways. You can work real hard and save up enough money to buy a seat in the upper deck. Or you can make sure you have a friend who will invite you to sit behind the third-base dugout.

It's totally up to you.

The first fight my dad and I had on "take your unlucky son to work day" was about what I was going to wear.

As soon as my dad told me I had to wear a tie, I demanded a raise to forty dollars.

"Denied," said my dad.

"No way!" I argued. "You know how the skin on my neck is so sensitive? How I get those rashes all the time?" He looked at me blankly, so I added, "A tie could quite possibly kill me."

Dad sighed the first of what would turn out to be many sighs that day and quickly decided that this was not a fight he wanted to have. "Fine, just wear a decent shirt that doesn't have a picture of a death metal band on it."

You may have thought I won that fight, but I didn't, since I still had to wear long pants.

The train was packed. I thought I liked *my* cell phone, but you should have seen these people. It's amazing they weren't all in neck braces, the way they stared down at their phones and iPads, typing away. There were even a few people actually *talking* on their phones, which apparently is a big no-no, based on the looks they were getting.

I slept on the train, obviously, since I'd woken up approximately five hours earlier than usual. I like to sleep until noon on non-school days. Doesn't everybody?

***

The walk from the train station to my dad's office was about ten minutes, which was nine minutes too long. The office was really fancy. It had a lot of desks, which happens to be my least favorite kind of furniture. There were tons of people running around looking busy, phones were ringing constantly, and there were books everywhere (scary!).

My favorite room in the office was definitely the kitchen, which had a huge candy jar and free soda.

The first thing my dad did was introduce me to all the people. I could tell who were the ones who worked for him by how enthusiastically they greeted me: "Great to meet you, Charlie Joe!" or, "So this is the Charlie Joe I've heard so much about!"

Then I met his boss, Mr. Felcher, who looked kind of like a mean version of my grandfather. He was on the phone, so he just looked up and waved, kind of like he was swatting a fly. Then he put his hand over the phone and whispered, "Make sure your old man puts in a full day's work."

Dad laughed like it was the best joke that had ever been told on the planet.

I also met my dad's assistant, Sheila, who wore glasses around her neck. The only other person I'd ever seen do that was Mrs. Sleep, the principal at my school. Sheila was one of these people who thinks you have to talk extra loud to kids, like English is our second language or something.

"WELCOME TO WEISSLER, SELLER, AND MC-COLLUM," she said, overenthusiastically.

"Who?" I asked.

"That's the name of the firm," my dad clarified, before Sheila had the chance to rattle my eardrums again.

"Oh," I said. "Are any of them around? I'd like to meet Weissler first, followed by Seller, and then McCollum."

"They've all passed away," my dad answered.

71

That seemed weird. Who would want to work at a company that was run by a bunch of dead guys?

"Mr. Jackson's office, please hold," Sheila said into the phone, before turning back to me. "NICE TO MEET YOU, CHARLE JOE. FEEL FREE TO COME TO ME FOR ANYTHING YOU NEED." She was nice. I could see how working wasn't so bad if you had someone around who would do anything you needed.

Maybe if you played your cards right, you could even get her to do the work for you.

Then two guys in suits and one woman in a woman suit came up to my dad.

"The brief and the motion and the verdict and the jury and the recess and the Judge!" they said. (Okay, I'm making that up—I don't exactly speak lawyer. But there was some sort of emergency—that much was clear.)

"Guys, give me one minute," my dad said. He turned to me, trying to figure out how to put me to work. Then he looked around his office and spotted a huge stack of papers about a mile high. Then he looked at me again.

"No way," I said.

"Charlie Joe, I need you to look through that document and find all the references to *Furman v. the State of Missouri*, circle them, and put a Post-it note on those pages."

Furman v. the State of Missouri? It sounded like a boxing match. And not a very fair fight.

"How long will that take?" I asked.

"Should take us right up until lunch," my dad said, gathering up a bunch of papers and books and notes and hurrying out the door. "We'll go someplace delicious, I promise."

"THERE'S A CHINESE PLACE RIGHT AROUND THE CORNER THAT I LOVE," Sheila screamed.

Well, that's good. Two hundred pages of lawyer stuff seemed a little less painful, knowing that a big plate of sesame chicken would be waiting on the other side.

21

I don't want to bore you by talking about how boring Furman was, and how boring the State of Missouri was (sorry Missouri people, I'm sure it's not your fault), and how I was so bored I started having little conversations with each piece of Post-it paper I used. ("There you go, little Posty, have a nice life on page seventeen.")

All you really need to know is that after about twenty pages (out of 237), I fell fast asleep on my dad's couch. I think I may have drooled a little bit on his pillow. It was a swell nap, until I was woken up by a sharp poke in the ribs.

Dad's boss, Mr. Felcher.

"Hard at work, I see," he grumbled. I figured I was supposed to laugh, so I did. But Mr. Felcher didn't seem all that amused. "Where's your father? We've got a problem."

"He went to judge a pair of briefs, or something like that," I said. Then I noticed Sheila standing at the door. She had that expression on her face that you see when people are watching a horror movie, and they don't want the cute girl to open the door to the basement.

"Judge a pair of briefs?" the old guy barked. "What does that even mean?"

My dad came running into the room. He saw three things that didn't exactly make him jump for joy: me lying on his couch, a drool mark on his pillow, and his boss perched over me like a mean, old crow.

"Were you looking for me?" my dad asked Mr. Felcher, but the old guy stomped away.

"We'll talk later at the partner meeting," he yelled back over his shoulder.

My dad stood there for a second, then slowly sank down on the couch next to me.

"I found thirteen Furmans before I fell asleep," I said, trying to look on the bright side.

"Maybe I should go into the dog-walking business," he answered.

* * *

We went to Sheila's Chinese place for lunch, where my dad tried to get mad at me for passing out on his couch. His heart wasn't in it, though, I think because he realized that no kid should be able to read a 237-page legal document without falling asleep at least six times.

Then he launched into a long story about how he wanted to be a writer when he was younger, but when he met my mom he realized he had to get a real job, so he went back to law school and became a lawyer, and usually he really likes it but sometimes he doesn't, but either way it's his job and he takes pride in how hard he works at it because our family depends on him, and my mom works just as hard at home because the family depends on her, too, and the sooner I realized the value of hard work, the better off I would be later in life.

I was too busy enjoying my sesame chicken to pay close attention, but I suddenly heard him loud and clear when he stopped talking.

He looked at me. "What do you think?"

I wasn't sure what exactly he was referring to, so I said the first thing that popped into my head.

"I think it's delicious."

He glared at me. "Did you even hear a word I said?"

This time he was able to stay mad.

My dad and I walked back to his office without talking, and when we got upstairs he said, "Just wait here and do whatever you want while I go to this meeting, then as soon as it's done we'll go home. Don't break anything."

I felt a little guilty that he didn't think I could last a whole day at his office, but I felt a lot psyched that I didn't have to spend a whole day at his office.

After about twenty minutes killing time on my dad's computer playing video games, my cell phone rang.

"Hey, Mom."

"Hi, honey! I need to ask Daddy a really important question, and he's not answering his phone. Is he with you?"

I knew he was in a meeting, but my mom needed him, and besides, I was looking for something to do. "I can find him, hold on."

I walked down the hall, peeking in rooms and offices, but no luck. Then I saw a door that said CONFERENCE ROOM and I remembered that he said he had a meeting. As far as I knew, meetings were probably like conferences, and they probably happened in conference rooms.

So I went in, and there he was. Along with about twenty other people, including Mr. Felcher.

They were all really, really dressed up, and they all looked really, really serious.

My dad looked up, saw me, and immediately turned the color of a tomato.

"What do you need, Charlie Joe," he said, although he didn't even really open his mouth when he said it.

"Um, Mom wants to talk to you."

My dad closed his eyes and took a deep breath. "Not now."

"Dad can't talk right now," I whispered into the phone, and hung up.

Just then Mr. Felcher smacked the laptop that was in front of him and said, "Damn these things!"

Well, that was kind of cool that he swore, but nobody else seemed to think it was all that cool, because everybody got even quieter, and they had all been pretty silent to begin with.

Then somebody said, "What's the problem with the laptop? Maybe I can help."

The room went even silent-er. Then, for some reason, everyone looked at me.

Which was when I realized that the "somebody" who had said that was me.

Mr. Felcher clapped his hands together. "So, Rip Van Winkle knows his way around a computer, does he?"

It seemed like he was waiting for an answer, so I said, "I guess."

"Well, come take a look," he said, waving me over. I walked up to Mr. Felcher and kind of stood there, until he looked at the guy in the suit sitting next to him and said, "Do you mind?" Whether the guy minded or not, he got up very quickly. I sat down in the chair and checked out his laptop. It was a sweet MacBook Pro. Jake Katz has one. He also has Hannah Spivero. I'm not sure which I want more. But that's beside the point.

Mr. Felcher pushed the computer in front of me. "I can't figure out why every time I try to read this document, it goes away and this godforsaken picture of my grandchildren pops up. I mean, I love those kids, but I don't want to look at them all day long." All the partners laughed, probably because they thought that if they didn't, they would soon be ex-partners.

For a second, I couldn't believe that he was asking me such a ridiculously simple question, and I almost laughed. But then by some miracle, I realized that laughing would have been very stupid. So I looked at his screen and acted as if he were dealing with a very difficult problem. "See, the problem is you think you're clicking on the document, but you're actually clicking right next to the document," I said, moving his mouse around the screen to show him. "When you click right next to the document, you're clicking on whatever file is underneath your document, which in this case happens to be a picture of your grandchildren, which you must have opened when somebody sent it to you in an e-mail. If you click in the middle of the file you want, you'll always stay on that file."

I handed the mouse back to Mr. Felcher, and he clicked on the picture, then clicked back on the file he wanted. When the correct file popped up, he let out a huge guffaw. "Well, take a look at that. Kid, you're a genius!"

Everybody murmured in amazement that such a complicated procedure could be accomplished on such an advanced machine in such a short period of time. What they were really thinking was, *If only I'd helped Mr. Felcher with that ridiculously easy problem, I'd be getting a sweet corner office right about now.*

The big boss took my hand and shook it so hard I thought

he was going to dislocate my shoulder. "These kids today," he said to the room, "just when you think they can't do anything right, they go ahead and amaze you." He looked at my dad. "Fine boy you've got here, Jackson—fine boy."

My dad hadn't moved a muscle since I entered the room, but somehow he managed to smile and nod. Then he immediately got up, and I knew he was thinking what I was thinking—we should probably end this day on a high note.

"Nice to meet everybody," I said to everyone in the room as we were leaving.

My dad shut the door, and as we walked down the hall he said to me, "That was the craziest thing I ever saw. Let's hit the road while I still have a job."

It seemed like a good time to cash in. "That was one sweet laptop," I said. "Can I get one of those?"

"In your dreams," said my dad. But he softened the blow by handing me the twenty bucks. "Here ya go. You earned it."

I stared down at the money. It felt good in my hands.

"For forty bucks, I'll come back tomorrow," I offered.

He laughed. "Wow, you're starting to sound like a real lawyer."

I slept the whole train ride home.

Charlie Joe's Financial Tip #5

JUST BECAUSE ADULTS WORK DOESN'T MEAN KIDS HAVE TO.

I support the idea of adults working. I really do, especially if it means they use some of the money they earn to occasionally buy you things. But why should that mean that kids have to work, too?

Here are just a few of the reasons why I think adults actually don't mind working:

1. *It gets them out of the house and away from their screaming kids.*
2. *It gets them out of the house and away from their annoying husband or wife.*
3. *It lets them buy nice things that they can use to show off in front of other adults.*
4. *It makes the weekends that much sweeter.*

Part Three
THE BAR AND THE MITZVAH

So it turned out that making money wasn't as easy as I thought. So far I'd had to deal with missing dogs, unlucky gophers, two-hundred-page documents, and mean bosses, and all I had to show for it was thirty-two lousy dollars. There had to be another way.

It took me a while, but eventually, I found one.

See, the thing is, you can come up with a way to make some real money when you absolutely, positively have to. And I was about to have to.

Why?

The same reason middle school boys have to do anything.

Middle school girls.

Katie here.

I took Charlie Joe's book back because we're getting to the part that's more about me, and I want to make sure it's accurate.

It's not that I don't trust Charlie Joe.

It's just that I trust myself more.

My band, CHICKMATE, is probably the most important thing in my life—which is why our gig at Jake's bar mitzvah was shaping up to be the most important night of my life.

I've wanted to be in a band ever since I first discovered classic rock. I wish I could say that my heroes growing up were Joan Jett, or Nancy Wilson from Heart, or Lady Gaga, or some other cool girl musician; but the truth is I was totally in love with, and wanted to be, Axl Rose. I can't help it, I just LOVE Guns N' Roses—even if they do have a somewhat checkered history with the opposite sex.

I don't judge them. I just listen to them.

But I'm not a moron, and I know a girl in middle school would maybe get committed to a mental hospital if she tried to form a band that sounded like GNR, so CHICK-MATE is a lot softer—we turn up the volume on the guitars sometimes, but generally we prefer to leave people with their eardrums intact. We play all famous songs, because that's what the people want to hear—but hopefully one day soon we'll start doing our own songs. Come on—people singing along to something I wrote? How amazing would THAT be?

Anyway, that's just a little background—I could go on for hours about our band, that's how obsessed I am—so you know how important Friday night's gig was.

Anyway, it was three days before the show, and the band was rehearsing—me, on guitar and vocals; Becca Clausen, on guitar and background vocals; Jackie Bender on keyboards; and Sammie Corcoran on drums. (We're still looking for a bass player, if you know anyone.) We were kind of stressed out, because we only knew like four songs and we were supposed to know eight.

Also, it was going to be only our second time performing in front of actual human beings.

We were about twenty minutes in, just starting to rock, when the door opened and Charlie Joe walked in.

"Why aren't you returning my calls?"

I looked at my phone—three missed calls—and waved it at him.

"It's kind of hard to hear a phone that's on vibrate when you're playing rock and roll."

"Is that what you call it?"

The other girls didn't like that.

"What do you want?" asked Sammie.

"Why are you here, Charlie Joe?" asked Becca.

Charlie Joe glanced around, as if he were just realizing other people were actually there. "This isn't about you guys."

Now the thing is, Becca is a very sweet person, and a very polite person. She's also a very tall person—about

five feet nine inches tall—and a star defender on the travel soccer team.

So when she got up and said to Charlie Joe, "We have an important gig coming up, and it's probably best if you leave so we can rehearse," he suddenly realized that it was very much about her, indeed.

He also realized that Sammie had two drumsticks in her hands.

"Okay, sorry, give me one quick second," Charlie Joe said, yanking me into the next room.

"You need to leave," I announced, having finally run out of patience with Charlie Joe Jackson and his shenanigans.

He ignored me. "I just wanted to let you know I discovered that money is overrated."

I had to laugh. "Wow. I'm so relieved."

"No, I'm serious," Charlie Joe said. "Sure, I'd love to have cool things like a Botman, but I'd rather just have

89

fun and enjoy life. And besides, why do people need to have something just because someone else has it? That kind of thinking might be exactly what's wrong with America."

Wow. Was this really Charlie Joe talking?

Then something occurred to me.

"How was going to work with your dad?"

Charlie Joe shook his head. "A real eye-opener. His office was full of books. His boss was the scariest person I've ever met in my life. And get this"—he shuddered like he just saw a ghost—"I almost had to wear a *tie*."

Ah, so *that* was it.

My bandmates started practicing again without me. "I HAVE TO GO REHEARSE," I shouted.

Then Charlie Joe did this weird thing. He kissed me on the cheek and gave me a big hug.

"I can't wait for the bar mitzvah," he said. "You guys are going to rock it OUT."

As Charlie Joe left, I realized I had a grin on my face that no self-respecting rock chick would ever have. It seemed like Charlie Joe had really turned the corner about trying to cut corners—if not in school, then at least in terms of making money.

I should have known better.

Hey, I got the book back.

Katie was getting a little too involved, so I finally had to put my foot down.

And when that didn't work, I begged and pleaded until she gave it back.

As the week went on, Jake's bar mitzvah became the main topic of conversation.

"I wish you weren't having a sports theme," Hannah told him at lunch on Wednesday. "I hate sports themes."

"Next bar mitzvah I'll have a princess theme," Jake responded.

Pete Milano scratched his head. "You're going to have another bar mitzvah?"

Poor Pete.

"I'll have to change in the car, since I'll be coming straight from lacrosse practice," Timmy chimed in, simply because he never missed an opportunity to remind everyone that he was on the travel team.

At the next table, Eliza's Botman made an announcement. "Yo, Spanish class in ten minutes. *Andale!*" Eliza laughed, scooped up her little toy, and stood up, which meant that the Elizettes—the three girls who did everything she did—got up, too.

They came over to our table.

"Charlie Joe, are you excited to hear Katie's band?" Eliza asked. All the guys looked at me bitterly, annoyed at the fact that for some reason, the prettiest girl in the grade still had a crush on me.

"I'm totally excited," I told Eliza. "Aren't you?"

Eliza stretched like a bored cat. "I'm not even sure I'll get there in time to see them," she purred. "I might be late, since I have a zillion things to do."

"Yeah, we might get there a little late," agreed the Elizettes.

Everyone stopped talking and looked at Eliza. This was big. This was a clear-cut statement, an example of an A-list girl not willing to share the spotlight with someone a little lower down on the food chain.

People seemed to be waiting for me to respond, so I said, "Why wouldn't you go? This is a big night for Katie and the other girls in the band, and we're all going to be there. Do your zillion things some other time."

I'm not even sure I'll get there in time to see them.

Eliza looked around. She was brave, but only up to a point, and she realized that this probably wasn't the best time to make whatever statement she was trying to make.

"I'll think about it," she said, and walked away.

We all took a second to recover from that tense moment. Then the conversation turned to the most crucial element of any successful bar mitzvah: the boy to girl ratio. Jake was extremely worried that another event across town—I think it was a confirmation—was going to steal away some of the girls.

Apparently he didn't want to become a man in front of a bunch of boys.

"Perhaps you should widen your pool of attendees to include those who might not otherwise meet your criteria, such as younger girls and older girls," said Nareem.

Jake shook his head. "It's a little late for that, don't you think? The bar mitzvah is in two days."

"Besides," I added, "you can't invite younger girls, that would be embarrassing. And older girls would laugh at Jake if he invited them. Nice try, Nareem."

Nareem sighed. He was a total genius, but he still had a few things to learn about the social rules of middle school.

"I don't see why you care about having more girls," said Hannah, with good reason. Jake was her boyfriend, and she probably wasn't thrilled about the idea of a bunch of girls swarming around him and treating him like the king of the world, which is what happens to the guest of honor at bar mitzvahs. "The girls you really know and care about will be there, and that should be enough, right?"

Timmy rolled his eyes. "It's not about Jake, it's about the rest of us. We need girls!"

"If there aren't enough girls there, I'm totally not giving you any money," Pete announced in his usual obnoxious way.

The bell rang, but we kept talking about it for another minute until Ms. Ferrell walked up. Ms. Ferrell was definitely my favorite adult at school—she was nice, she was funny, and she was always encouraging, even after the somewhat awkward dog-walking episode. The only annoying habit she had was when she interrupted a very important conversation just because we were in school. That happened all the time, and I have to tell you, it gets old after a while.

"Hi, guys. Not to butt in or anything, but since you are actually at school, I thought maybe you could try going to class and doing some actual learning."

Katie looked embarrassed. She wasn't used to being disciplined by any teacher, much less Ms. Ferrell, who totally loved her.

But her reaction was nothing compared to Nareem's, who looked like he thought he was going to get thrown in jail. "I'm so very sorry, Ms. Ferrell," he said. "This was inexcusable behavior. I am not sure what came over me."

Ms. Ferrell smiled. "You're a boy, Nareem. That's what came over you."

"**Explain to me again** what a dance wrangler is?" my dad said.

It was the night before Jake's bar mitzvah, and we were sitting at dinner. My dad was shocked that people were actually paid to get kids to dance.

Megan rolled her eyes. "Daddy, when's the last time you were at a bar mitzvah or a confirmation party or a school dance? Or any social event with a bunch of middle school kids? At the beginning of the night all the boys stand on one side and all the girls on the other, just staring at each other like there's some huge ocean between them. You need the dance wranglers to break the ice. Then once everyone is out there, it's all good. Let the grinding begin."

My dad dropped his fork. "Grinding?"

"You don't want to know," my mother said.

"Can we talk about something else?" I said.

My mom looked at me. "Aren't you hungry?"

I was pushing my food around the plate, which drove Moose and Coco crazy. They were thinking, *If you're just going to play with your food, give it to US! We know what to do with it.*

I finally gave up and put my fork down. "I should proba-bly get to bed. Big day tomorrow." My dad dropped his knife this time. The last time I'd voluntarily gone to bed this early was . . . let's see . . . never.

"'Night," I said, and headed up to my room. I'd been there approximately one second when there was a knock at the door and Megan came in.

"Dude," she said, "what's up with you?"

I sat down on the bed. "What do you mean?"

But I knew exactly what she meant. Because Megan knew my dirty little secret. The night before bar mitzvahs, I got a little freaked out—for one, big reason.

I was a lousy dancer.

She sat down next to me. "Charlie Joe, listen to me. You gotta dial down the whole nervous thing." Megan was not only an excellent older sister, she was also a girl—like most sisters—and so she was able to give me some inside information on what being a girl was all about. "Girls don't care if you're a good dancer or not. They just care if you're funny and sweet while you try not to step on their toes."

I tried to smile. "Seriously?"

Megan giggled. "Seriously. But that doesn't mean they won't make fun of you a little. Girls are girls, after all. That's what makes us fun."

I flopped back on the bed. "That's one word for it, I suppose."

Megan bopped me on the head with a pillow. "Get your beauty sleep, Fred Astaire."

I had no idea who Fred Astaire was, but I fell asleep anyway.

A bar mitzvah usually comes in two parts. In the morning, way before you would ordinarily get up on a weekend, you have to sit in a temple for two hours trying to avoid being yelled at by adults for talking, while watching your friend say a bunch of stuff in a foreign language that's impossible to understand.

The reward for surviving that part is the party at night, where the girls are in pretty dresses, the music is deafening, and the desserts are life-changing.

During the morning service, I was still kind of quiet, nervously thinking about dancing. The parents all complimented me for being uncharacteristically well-behaved.

When I walked into the party, though, the first thing I saw was the dessert table, and I cheered up immediately. (At some bar mitzvahs—the good ones—the dessert table is out all night. Dinner becomes kind of an afterthought.) Along with the chocolate fountain, which is an old standby and was its usual magnificent self, there was this awesome make-your-own-popcorn-sundae bar, called Pop-a-palooza. You get a bucket of popcorn, and then you have your choice of a bunch of toppings: melted chocolate, melted marshmallow, melted toffee, melted caramel—it was heaven. None of us had ever seen a popcorn sundae bar before, and we were all kind of mesmerized by it, in a good way.

I'd eaten about four pounds of chocolate popcorn when the lights went down and the screaming started.

Suddenly a loud chord jolted the room, the lights went back up, and there was Katie's band.

The first thing I noticed was that I'd never seen Katie so happy. The second thing was that her band was good. I mean, REALLY good. I mean, if I didn't know better I would have said that Katie Friedman was going to be a rock star one day. The music was intense and catchy—and if you ask me, intense and catchy are the major food groups of good music.

They did about five songs, then Katie said, "We're CHICKMATE, thanks for listening! Coming up next, Spinster the DJ."

Then she raised a cup of soda. "A big shout-out to Jake Katz, the bar mitzvah boy!" She was a natural—it was like she'd been giving shout-outs to bar mitzvah boys all her life.

Everyone went wild as CHICKMATE left the stage. The girls in the band were so freaked out by how much people liked them that they didn't know what to do, so they just jumped on each other and screamed. Even polite, reserved, but huge and therefore still scary Becca Clausen, the rhythm guitar player, squealed like a five-year-old girl.

Katie hugged Nareem, then came over to talk to me.

"So?" she said, grinning from ear to ear.

I didn't really know what to say. I was just so impressed, and proud of her, and proud to be her friend, and feeling so cool that I was the first person she came over to that I literally just stood there, shaking my head and smiling.

Katie punched my arm. "Wow, you're totally speechless. I don't think I've ever seen that before. That bad, huh?"

But she was laughing. She knew exactly what I was thinking.

Just as I managed to stammer, "That was incredible," I was immediately drowned out by the unmistakable scream of a middle-school-aged girl bearing down on us at top speed.

I turned to see who it was, expecting one of the usual suspects—one of Katie's kind of weird friends, who wear black sweaters and odd-shaped glasses and stuff—but instead found myself face-to-face with a blast from the past.

Zoe Alvarez.

Yup.

That Zoe Alvarez.

Let me back up a minute: Zoe Alvarez is the girl who almost became my girlfriend, until she moved away at the end of last year.

She was also the *first* girl in the world who made me

realize that Hannah Spivero wasn't necessarily the *only* girl in the world.

I hadn't seen Zoe in like five months, but I still thought about her every once in a while. Okay, fine—slightly more than every once in a while.

Our eyes met, and it was immediately weird. I'd spent a lot of time wondering what I would say to her the next time I saw her, but now that she was actually standing right in front of me, I couldn't come up with a single word. And I think she was having the same problem. So we ended up having a staring contest. It seemed like thirty seconds, but was probably more like five.

She gave up first, by turning to Katie and giving her a huge girly hug and letting out a huge girly scream. Then they talked a mile a minute to each other about how awesome it was to see each other.

"Jake called me earlier today with this awesome idea to invite Zoe," Katie announced. "He was still worried about having enough girls. And she came! Isn't that awesome?"

I looked at Zoe, she looked at me, and finally we did this weird half-hug thing. "Wow, cool. It's really great to see you, Zoe."

Zoe flashed that smile I remembered from the first time I met her, in Mrs. Massey's art studio. "Katie's been filling me in on everything," she said. "She says you're still always asking her for advice, and she still bails you out over and over again."

It took me a minute to wrap my head around the fact that Katie and Zoe had been in touch the last couple of months. I thought Katie told me everything. Guess not.

"Some things never change," I said.

"Yup," Zoe said, before she was dragged away to say hi to some other old friends.

Hmm, I thought to myself. *This is turning out to be an interesting night.*

When the DJ took over, I headed straight back to the Pop-a-palooza, which seemed like the perfect place to avoid dancing. Pete Milano joined me, and we were in the middle of stuffing our faces with melted goodness when the first dance wranglers appeared.

"You guys ready to boogie?" asked one dance wrangler, a pretty curly-haired girl who had some sort of earring in her belly button.

"I'm totally ready to boogie!" Pete Milano replied, spilling some of his sticky popcorn all over the floor. He looked down, thought about it for a second, then scooped it up and ate it.

"Five-second rule, dudes," Pete mumbled through a mouthful of popcorn and dust.

"Ew, gross," said a voice behind us.

I turned around—Zoe.

Uh-oh.

Standing there with Hannah Spivero.

Double uh-oh.

Hannah and Zoe hadn't exactly been best friends when Zoe went to school with us. I'd like to think that it was because Hannah was jealous of Zoe, but that would be giving myself too much credit.

"Look who I ran into," Zoe yelled to me over the music.

"That's great," I yelled back. "She's worth running into."

Zoe put her arm around Hannah, as if to make sure there were no leftover hard feelings. "She told me she's still going out with Jake, isn't that awesome?"

"Couldn't be awesome-er," I said.

"Do you want to dance?" Zoe asked me, out of the blue.

It took me a minute to answer, even though I shouldn't have been surprised by the request. Zoe was never the shy type. I tried to think of an excuse, but then realized for the first time in my life, I actually wanted to dance.

"Okay."

We got out there and shuffled around for a few minutes without saying anything.

"You're a good dancer," Zoe said finally.

"Very funny," I answered, and she laughed.

After a few more (mis)steps, Zoe said, "I'm sorry I didn't write you back over the summer. I kind of knew my parents were getting back together, and that I'd be moving back to my dad's house, and I wasn't sure how to tell you. That was really lame."

"It's totally fine," I said, momentarily forgetting how totally unfine I thought it was at the time. "How's your year going so far?"

"Pretty good."

"Mine, too."

We semidanced for another minute or so, and then Zoe spoke again. "Are you still totally in love with Hannah?"

Luckily the song ended right there, and I could clap instead of answering.

✷ ✷ ✷

Then it was time for the slide show, which was a twenty-minute tribute to the guest of honor: baby pictures, family pictures, school pictures, vacation pictures, goofy pictures, sports pictures.

Considering Jake was the guest of honor, I was kind of surprised there were no reading pictures.

I was sitting there, pretending to thoroughly enjoy myself, when I felt a tug on my arm. "Come on, let's go," someone whispered.

I turned around to see Zoe squatting down behind me. She pulled my arm again.

"This is boring," she said a little bit louder. I think she was losing the patience required to whisper. "Let's go get a soda."

"*Sssssh!*" someone said. I looked around at all the other kids who were sitting on the floor, being good little children and quietly watching the tribute to Jake, knowing that it was a small sacrifice to make for all the dancing, jumping, eating, drinking, and flirting to follow. Then I looked back at the screen, which was scrolling through an adorable group of pictures that showed Jake winning first prize at the tri-county science fair for some experiment that involved a hamster, a Ping-Pong ball, some superglue, and a large block of cheese.

I decided to make a run for it.

I scrambled to my feet and followed Zoe out to the main hall, trying to ignore all the heads swiveling in our direction. I felt like an outlaw fleeing a bank robbery. I have to admit, it was a pretty good feeling.

We headed over to the bar.

"Scotch and soda, hold the soda," I said to the guy serving drinks. Zoe laughed, which gave me a warm feeling inside.

"You mean hold the scotch," said the guy, who was obviously born without a sense of humor.

He poured us a couple of cokes.

Zoe clinked my glass. "I'm really glad Katie called me to come to Jake's bar mitzvah."

"I'm glad, too," I said. "And I'm extra glad you actually came."

I hate it when the truth sounds lame.

We headed outside to the lawn. Since the theme of Jake's bar mitzvah was baseball (sports was by far the favorite theme for boys; girls were all over the map, with pop stars and nightclubs being two of the leaders), the whole outside of the club was decorated with bleachers and flags and artificial turf. There was even a hot dog stand and a batting cage.

"I love batting!" Zoe said, spotting the cage. "Let's go bat some balls." Then she took my hand and led me over.

Let me repeat that: THEN SHE TOOK MY HAND.

(I should probably stop here and point out that while I may talk a good game, and occasionally try to sound like I know what I'm doing in terms of girls, this was maybe the fourth time a girl had ever taken my hand voluntarily. As opposed to being forced to, on some third grade field trip.)

Zoe got into the batting cage and started smashing balls all over the place. She was a regular girl Babe Ruth. (Hannah was also a girl Babe Ruth. Why did I always fall for girl Babe Ruths?) The batting cage guy and I just stood there, staring at her with our mouths open.

After twenty pitches, she handed the bat to me. "Your turn."

Oh, fantastic.

I swung and missed. Then I swung and missed again. Then I foul-tipped one.

"Nice!" Zoe yelled.

Finally, on the fourth pitch, I got ahold of one! Kind of. It dribbled weakly up the middle and came to a gentle stop underneath the pitching machine.

"Sweet!" Zoe screamed.

I decided to quit while I was ahead and I handed the bat to the guy. "We should probably go inside before the slide show ends," I said, but Zoe was already at the hot dog stand, ordering two with everything. She took the first one and ate it in two bites. Then she handed the other one to me and did a cartwheel, a back handspring, and two roundoffs.

Right then, it occurred to me that girls were fascinating, unknowable creatures.

We sat down in the fake dugout and didn't say anything for a minute or two. Then she turned to look at me. "Charlie Joe, remember at the end of last year, when you kissed Hannah on stage during the school play?"

My face turned red. Remember? How could I ever forget? First of all, there was the fact that the entire town was watching. Second of all, there was the fact that I'd panicked and run off stage right before the big moment. And third of all, there was the fact that I'd finally gotten my act together and KISSED HANNAH! (Well, technically, she'd kissed me, before I had a chance to wimp out again.)

"Yeah, I remember."

Zoe leaned in closer.

"Well, I kind of wished that it was me up there with you."

I looked at her. She looked like she was waiting for me to do something. Maybe even kiss her. And I wanted to do it, I really did. But for some reason, I hesitated—just like in the play, with Hannah.

"I wish you would just make up your mind," Zoe said, annoyed.

Then she ran back inside, leaving me standing there, trying to make up my mind about what she meant by making up my mind.

31

Every middle school party goes on about twenty minutes too long, and Jake's Big Baseball Bar Mitzvah Bash was no exception. By the time we'd all eaten dessert, eaten dinner, eaten a second dessert, jump danced a lot, maybe slow danced a little, grinded when the adults weren't looking, watched the slide show, used the batting cage, posed for pictures with some professional minor league baseball player nobody had ever heard of, and eaten a third dessert, everyone was completely wiped out. The only thing left to do was to wait for our parents to pick us up.

A bunch of us decided to go outside and hang out in the bleachers. Now that the dancing was over, boys and girls separated again—boys on one bleacher, girls on the other. The boys were using their ties as whips and having whipping fights. The girls, who because of some weird fashion thing were forced to wear unbelievably uncomfortable shoes, were sitting down and rubbing their feet.

The only kid missing was Jake, who was inside with his relatives, getting kissed on the top of his head a lot.

I was still replaying the Zoe conversation in my head,

where she basically said she wanted to kiss me. Wow. I started thinking . . . she didn't really live that far away . . . we could maybe see each other on weekends . . . try another double date with Jake and Hannah (the last one didn't go so well, BTW) . . . in other words, actually *be boyfriend and girlfriend*.

"Zoe Alvarez," Pete said, reading my mind.

"Yeah," I answered.

He snorted. "She totally still wants you. She was giving you a tonsillectomy with her eyes."

"Stop being a turd," I told him.

Timmy came up to me and smacked me with his tie— which was a clip-on, by the way. "This was a pretty good party." He was feeling good because Kelly Gaspers, a girl he liked, said that he was "getting cuter every day."

"Charlie Joe thought it was a great party, too," Pete said. "Didn't you, lover boy?"

Timmy smirked. "So what's the deal with Zoe? Are you two going to pick up where you left off?"

"I doubt it," I said. "Girls are weird."

That launched a whole long conversation about how annoying girls could be—a topic that never gets old.

Pete was in the middle of telling us one of his random theories—this one was something about how girls only like guys who get only one haircut a year—when Katie came over to our side of the bleachers.

"What are you guys talking about?"

"Girls," said Timmy.

"Mostly one girl in particular," added Pete, elbowing me in the ribs.

Katie laughed. "I knew it. If you two got together once and for all, that would be so great. It's time you officially got over Hannah anyway."

"Really?" I asked.

"Really, really."

"But Zoe lives in Kenwood."

Katie swatted me on the arm. "And you live in Eastport. So what? Don't be a dolt."

I looked at her and thought I saw a tiny trace of irritation cross her face. Or maybe it was jealousy? The jealous face was something I was familiar with, since I saw it in the mirror every day last summer, when I was jealous of Katie and Nareem at Camp Rithubukkee. It was really weird: Katie and I had always been best friends, and everyone knows that best friends and romance don't mix; so the fact that I'd been jealous of her last summer, and she might be jealous of me now, made absolutely no sense.

But since when does life make sense?

"Okay, fine," I said.

I went over to the girls' bleachers and walked up to Zoe, heart pounding. After a second, she looked up at me.

"Hi," she said.

Amazing how one simple word can make your heart start beating normally again.

"Hi," I said back.

"It was great hanging out with you again," Zoe said. "We should stay in touch this time."

I nodded. "We totally should."

Cars were starting to pull into the parking lot. The official end of the night. We kept an eye out, but neither of our parents were there yet. A few more minutes.

Suddenly she looked back at me.

"So, this is totally crazy, but do you maybe want to come visit me sometime this year?"

"Definitely," I said. "Kenwood is only like twenty minutes away."

Zoe smiled. "Yeah, well, that's the thing. I'm not going to be in Kenwood. In like a month we're moving to Ohio, to be closer to my grandparents. I'm not going to know anybody, obviously, so I'm hoping some friends will come visit me. Do you think maybe you could?"

Wait. *What the what?*

I stared at her. "Seriously? You're moving *again?*"

"I know," she said. "I'd never moved before in my life and now I'm about to move for the second time in a year!"

"Why didn't you say anything?" I asked in shock. I wanted to add, *Like out at the batting cages, when you basically said you wished I'd kissed you, but I didn't.*

Zoe looked at her feet. "I didn't know how to tell you, I guess."

"Well, yeah, no," I said. "There's no way my parents

would let me go somewhere by myself. Especially to visit a girl."

"I totally get it," Zoe said quickly. "I shouldn't have brought it up, it was a stupid idea."

"Not stupid. Just not realistic."

Neither of us said anything for a minute.

Zoe took a deep breath. "It was really fun seeing you, though. I'm really going to miss you. All over again."

And she gave me a big hug.

Great, I thought. *Another thing to lie awake in bed thinking about.*

A car horn blew, and we all looked up.

"My mom," Zoe said.

She started walking to her car. As I watched her go, I got this really strong, weird feeling that I was never going to see her again. And then I got this even stronger, weirder feeling that I really, really didn't want that to happen.

"I would love to come visit you," I said.

She stopped. "You would? For real? What about your parents?"

I shrugged. "The least I can do is ask."

"Oh, Charlie Joe!" Zoe ran back, grabbed me, and gave me the longest hug I've ever gotten in my life. Or at least it was in the top ten of long hugs. (My mom had the other nine spots.) "That would be so totally totally amazing! I'll send you all the details!" Then she hugged Katie. "It was so great seeing you guys!"

We watched Zoe run to her mom's car. As they drove away, Katie turned to me.

"Did I hear that correctly? You're going to ask your parents if you can go visit Zoe Alvarez in Ohio?"

"She's awesome," I said, which wasn't exactly an answer to either of her questions.

"Well, good for you," Katie said. "There's only one small problem with your incredibly romantic plan."

"What's that?"

She gave me one of her legendary eye rolls.

"Everything."

My parents didn't say yes.

They didn't even said no.

What my dad actually said at breakfast the next morning was, "You're kidding, right? This is insane, even for you."

"You're in middle school," my mom added. "Middle school boys don't fly halfway across the country to visit middle school girls."

"It's not that crazy," I said. "Other kids are going to visit her."

"Like who?" my dad demanded.

"Like Katie," I said, even though technically that wasn't exactly, completely true.

"Oh, for God's sake," my mother said. "Where would you even get the money to do something like that?"

"Right," I said. "So, I was kind of hoping you might help out with that part."

My dad laughed so hard, I think a piece of bacon flew out of his nose.

I waited until he was done, then I said, "Okay, so I guess that's out."

"I'll tell you what," my dad said, drying his eyes. "You've been on this kick lately about making money. Well, now's your chance. You figure out a way to make yourself enough money to buy a plane ticket, and I'll let you go visit that friend of yours."

"Are you sure?" said my mom.

My dad snorted again, but this time, it was baconless. "Yeah, I'm sure. I think we're on pretty solid ground here, considering the plane ticket alone is going to cost around five hundred dollars."

Five hundred dollars?

Nice knowing you, Zoe.

33

"You're nuts," Jake said.

We were sitting in Jake's kitchen two days after his bar mitzvah, plowing through a bucket of fried chicken while I blabbed on about the whole Zoe-moving-to-Ohio-and-my-going-to-visit-her thing.

I chomped on a wing. "So you think I should just forget it?"

I think he said, "That's a tough one," but I couldn't be sure, since his mouth was full. So I waited until he finished, then asked again.

Jake took a swig of root beer. "Well, like I said, you're insane, but I definitely think you should go if you can," he said. "Zoe is so cool and she likes you, and you're obviously like totally in love with her."

"I wouldn't go that far," I said. *Obviously totally in love* sounded a little pathetic, although I suppose I could understand why Jake thought that.

"Whatever."

"But the really crazy part is that my parents said they would let me go," I told him. "All I have to do is pay for it myself."

Jake laughed. "Which basically means, they said forget it."

I nodded sadly. "Yeah, I guess so."

We ate in silence for a minute, as I thought about the situation. I'd never turned down a challenge from my parents, and I didn't want to start now. Even a challenge that was completely impossible.

"There's got to be a way for me to make some money," I said to Jake.

"Not some money," he corrected me. "A lot of money."

I nodded. "Right. And it has to be something that doesn't involve dogs, gophers, or lawyers."

"Somebody somewhere must need a mattress tester," Jake said.

"I would so do that."

He laughed. "Too bad you don't have a bar mitzvah coming up."

I looked up. "What does that have to do with it?"

Jake wiped his face with his shirt (How come there's never a napkin around when you need one?) and stood up. "Wait till you see this," he announced. Then he grabbed a big manila envelope, turned it up side down, and proceeded to dump about 6,347 checks onto his kitchen table.

I stared in shock. "Are you kidding me?"

Jake grinned. "I know, right? Suddenly all those mornings in Hebrew school don't seem so bad."

I picked up one check. It was from some people named Herman and Sheila Bergstein, and it was for one hundred dollars. I picked up another, from Paul Milano (Pete's dad), for thirty-six dollars, which for some weird reason was the traditional amount you were supposed to give. I picked up a third, from Betty Rosner, for fifty dollars.

And on and on and on and on.

When I thought about it for a second, it made complete sense. If my parents are writing a check, obviously so are everyone else's parents. Meanwhile, relatives are writing even bigger checks.

Holy moly. So THIS was how to make money.

Now, it's not like it was free money, which is what I was after. Jake had to work for his payday, and work hard. Hebrew school was a job, and a tough job, three days a week, for probably like five years.

Come to think of it, if you divided the money he made

at his bar mitzvah by the amount of time he spent at Hebrew school, the hourly rate probably wasn't even that great.

But still . . . like I said, holy moly.

"How much money is this?" I asked, lovingly cradling a bunch of checks in my arms.

"I have no idea," Jake said. "A boatload."

"More like a whole navy."

Eating helped me think, so I helped myself to another piece of chicken. Something was spinning in my head, but I couldn't quite get at it. It was like a trying to touch the rim on an eight-foot basket—just out of reach.

I ate my chicken, thinking, until the basket in my mind got lower. And then it got even lower. And then it got low enough so that I could touch the rim.

And then it got low enough so I could jam that basketball right through.

"I GOT IT!" I screamed. In my excitement I spit a tiny piece of fried chicken skin onto the table, which completely grossed Jake out. But I didn't care. I'd solved my problem.

"You got what?" Jake asked, trying not to gag.

"I finally figured out how to make a lot of money without working," I yelled, as proud of myself as I'd ever been in my entire life.

"This I gotta hear."

I held Jake's envelope over my head like it was the Super Bowl, World Series, and NBA Finals trophies all rolled into one.

"I'm going to have a bar mitzvah!"

I started racing around the room shouting, "I'm rich!" and, "Zoe here I come!" Jake watched me, munching quietly on his chicken, until he offered the only reasonable response to my grand plan.

"But you're not Jewish."

Charlie Joe's Financial Tip #6

NEVER MAKE EXTRA WORK FOR YOURSELF.

It's hard enough doing all the work you have to do just to get by in the world. So why would you create any extra?

If you have to read two books over the summer, pick short books. If you have to pick up your clothes off the floor, use a ski pole. If you have to mow the lawn, move to a house with a small yard.

Do what you have to do, what you're supposed to do, and not a thing more. Save your energy for the big stuff. Like eating and resting.

Part Four
THE BOY AND THE COW

So who would have thought my super-cool friend Charlie Joe could act like a lovesick puppy?

Sure, he'd been infatuated with Hannah for all those years, but he'd never done anything crazy about it. He just kept it to himself, except for the occasional comment to Jake, like "The fact that Hannah likes you and not me is proof that there is no logic to the universe."

But this was a whole new level.

All of a sudden Charlie Joe announces to a girl whom he hasn't seen in months that he's going to fly halfway across the country to visit her. How is he going to pull that off? Who's he going to go with? Where's he going to get the money? Has he thought about any of those things?

Of course not.

Charlie Joe doesn't work that way. He comes up with some grand idea and worries about the details later.

And usually, it's those details that get him into trouble.

Why do I have the feeling that this time won't be any different?

Okay, I'll give you back to Charlie Joe now.

35

Thanks for the vote of confidence, Katie.

Remember how we started, way back at
the beginning of the book? How I loved having money,
but hated having to work for it? How I loved having stuff,
but hated having to pay for it?

How I wanted a Botman so badly that I wound up ruin-
ing a gopher's day?

And then remember the middle part? When I saw Zoe
again at Jake's bar mitzvah, and we really hit it off *again*,
only for her to tell me that she was moving *again*? Then I
had my brilliant but crazy idea of going to Ohio to visit
her, and my dad actually saying I could go, as long as I figured out a way to pay for it?

(Of course you remember that last part, because it just
happened.)

Well, all of that was a mere warm-up to the payoff:
pretty much the best idea anyone ever had in terms of
making money.

Because not only was I going to make money, I was going
to make money by not working! By having fun. By throwing a party. By being the center of attention.

By having a bar mitzvah.

* * *

The first thing I had to figure out was how to get around the whole not-being-Jewish thing.

Back at school, I assembled the brain trust at lunch: Timmy, Nareem, Jake, and Hannah. Pete Milano was there, too, but he's more of a brain drain than a brain trust.

Katie sat reading a book, texting, and chiming in with the occasional eye-roll.

"This is going too far, Charlie Joe, even for you," she said at one point.

Fine, be that way.

"So I'm going to have a bar mitzvah," I announced to the group, ignoring the giggles. "Obviously, I'm not Jewish. But that shouldn't be a problem, since I'm not going to do the synagogue part anyway." People seemed confused by this, so I explained further. "I'm just going to do the party part."

More confusion.

"The part where people give you checks," Jake clarified.

"Correct," I confirmed.

Nareem scratched his head. "So if I am to understand this correctly, Charlie Joe, you plan on having a bar mitzvah, but you don't plan on actually preparing for, or following through on, the religious aspect of the ritual.

You only plan on reaping the financial benefits of such an occasion?"

I nodded. "You pretty much nailed it, Nareem."

He shook his head. "I'm not quite sure if you're incredibly clever or incredibly stupid."

"Or both," Jake suggested.

"I have to tell you, Charlie Joe," said Nareem, "I find your plan extremely risky and perhaps ill-advised."

Pete Milano didn't think it was ill-advised at all. In fact, he seemed awed by the plan. "Dude, you're gonna be rich. I should totally do that."

Wanting to steal your idea was the highest compliment Pete Milano could pay a person.

"So, Charlie Joe," Hannah said.

I looked at her, just like someone would look at a regular person. Seeing Zoe again made me able to look at Hannah without being blinded by her glorious aura. What a relief.

"Yeah?"

Hannah wrinkled her nose. (In the old days I got a little dizzy when she did that.) "I get that you're not having a religious ceremony," she said. "But you can't call it a bar mitzvah, right? I mean, isn't that only for Jewish people?"

"Hey, yeah," Pete said, showing some skepticism about my plan for the first time.

"That's true," I said. "I thought of that. Which is where you guys come in."

"Oh, great," muttered Timmy, who'd seen my ideas go wrong one too many times.

I ignored him. "I can't call it a bar mitzvah. I can't call it a confirmation, because I'm not doing the church part."

"Church has awesome cookies," Pete said, which didn't have anything to do with anything.

"Where my parents come from, they practice what is called the Sacred Thread ceremony," Nareem said. We all looked at him, so he went on. "I don't know anything about it, really, except that it's how a boy becomes a man. Do you want me to look it up on Wikipedia?"

"No thanks, I'm not into sewing," I said. "But you're on the right track, Nareem. I need to find some sort of weird, foreign ceremony that nobody has heard of, that I can make my thing."

"The Sacred Thread ceremony is not weird," Nareem objected.

"But it is foreign," I said. "And I need something even foreigner than that, if possible."

"More foreign," corrected Jake.

"Whatever."

Everyone thought for a minute, but it became clear pretty quickly that none of us had a lot of experience with ceremonies in which a boy becomes a man.

"I can't think of anything," Pete said, stating the obvious.

"That's okay," I said. "That's what the Internet is for."

Timmy and Jake had cell phones, so they immediately

went to work. It turns out there are plenty of ways for a boy to become a man out there in the world. For example:

Genpuku—in Japan, kids get adult clothes and adult haircuts. Didn't seem dramatic enough.

Poy Sang Long—in Thailand, boys have to become monks for a while before they become men. That wasn't going to work for me.

Rumspringa—where Amish boys get to experience the outside world before becoming men. Which actually sounds awesome, if you can ignore the fact that the Amish don't use electricity, meaning no television, video games, or blenders to make milkshakes. Sorry, that's a deal-breaker.

It was kind of fascinating and scary, all the ways boys became men—some of them were pretty freaky, and a few were extremely inappropriate for a thirteen-year-old, if you ask me.

But so far, none of them were going to help me get paid.

"This is quite educational, Charlie Joe, but so far nothing seems the slightest bit practical for your purposes," Nareem said.

"Besides, lunch is just about over," Hannah added, "and I've got to walk all the way to Health."

"We can't give up yet," I begged, but everyone started to gather up their stuff and get ready to go.

Then Timmy said, "Hey, has anyone ever heard of the Hamar?"

We all looked at Nareem, because if anyone had, he had. But he shook his head.

"What's the Hamar?" asked Jake.

Timmy was scrolling furiously on his phone. "It says here the Hamar are a tribal people who live in Southern Ethiopia."

"Cool. Ethiopia," Pete said. "That's a country, right?"

"It's a country in Africa," Nareem said.

"I thought Africa was a country," Pete responded.

Poor Pete.

"What *about* the Hamar?" I asked Timmy, trying to get back to the subject at hand.

"Well, they have a pretty cool thing that boys do to become men."

He stopped, relishing the moment, since he had everyone's attention now. Especially mine.

"Tell us," Hannah said.

"Tell us," Jake said.

"Would you mind please telling us," Nareem said.

Timmy stood up to make his big announcement. "Cow jumping."

"Cow jumping?" I said.

"Cow jumping?" Jake and Hannah said.

"Cow jumping?" Nareem said.

"You mean jumping over a freakin' cow?" Pete said, putting it another way.

Timmy nodded, feeling the glow of a triumphant discovery. "Yup, cow jumping. It says right here on Wikipedia that for the Hamar tribe, cow jumping is 'a rite of passage for men coming of age, as a symbol of the childhood he is about to leave behind him.'"

My mind started spinning. Cow jumping. That sounded like something I could do. That sounded like a party I could throw.

"Don't even think about it, Charlie Joe," Katie said, reading my mind as usual.

"There's nothing to think about," I said. "I'm in."

The bell rang for the end of lunch. We all picked up our backpacks, except for Timmy, who was still staring at his phone.

"Oh, there's one more thing," he said, in a way that made it clear that whatever the one more thing was, I wasn't going to be too happy about it.

We all stopped. "What's that?" I asked.

"You have to do it naked."

Pete Milano laughed so loud the lunch ladies dropped their fish sticks.

So it was official: I had a cow-jumping party to throw, and not a lot of time to get it organized. I had to move fast.

First stop was my sister Megan.

The next night after dinner, I waited until the last thing she would want to do was have a conversation with me. Then I started a conversation with her.

"Megan, you know how Mom and Dad are going away to dad's college reunion next month?"

She didn't look up from her texting. "Yeah?"

"Well, I had this idea."

This got her semi-attention. "Hold on a sec." First she had to finish her text. Then we had to sit there for about twenty seconds. Then she had to receive a return text that made her laugh.

Then I had her full attention. "What's your idea?"

This wasn't going to be easy. I cleared my throat. "So, you know how you're always saying that you and I should throw a party together some day, that your friends and my friends would get along great if they ever found themselves in the same room?"

Megan looked confused. Probably because she'd never said anything like that in her life.

"What are you talking about? You want to have a party?"

I put my arm around her. "I want *us* to have a party."

Her phone was buzzing. She was getting all sorts of texts and tweets and Instagrams and Snapchats, and I could tell she was dying to end her conversation with me and return to her conversations with half the eleventh grade.

In other words, it was the perfect time to make my move.

"Anyway, my idea is that when Mom and Dad go away to the college thing, that you and I throw a totally fun party. What do you think?"

She tried to process my request, which on the face of it was pretty ridiculous. When's the last time a high school sister and a middle school brother threw a party together? I think it was on the twelfth. The twelfth of Never.

Her phone buzzed again. She couldn't decide who to answer—her brother or the phone.

Finally she went for the phone. (They all do.) But before she started texting, she glanced up at me quickly. "I'll think about it," she said.

I took that as a yes.

Kids can surprise you sometimes.

Take Pete Milano, for example. He's one of the most immature kids you'll ever meet, gets in trouble all the time, totally annoying and loud and occasionally funny, but usually just obnoxious.

But, here's the weird thing—he's an amazing artist.

I remember when we were in our kindergarten art class and he was driving the teacher completely nuts, then she tells us to draw our pets, and he does this picture of himself next to his giant St. Bernard who had just died a couple of months earlier, and it was so beautiful it made the teacher cry.

Then in third grade I asked him to draw a picture of Hannah Spivero for me, which he did, and it was fantastic. I was so happy to give it to her, and when she took it she smiled at me, and I remember feeling about as happy as a human being can feel.

Then she turned it over and saw something on the back. She flung the picture back in my face and stomped off.

I picked up the drawing and looked on the back. Pete had written, *Dear Hannah. Here's a picture of your perfect face. Maybe one day I can kiss it with my tongue. Love, Charlie Joe Jackson.*

Like I said, sometimes kids can surprise you.

✳ ✳ ✳

But the point I'm trying to make is, Pete is an amazing artist.

Which is why I was trying to keep up with him as he ran around at recess throwing a Nerf football at all the girls.

"I need you to design the invitation to my cow-jumping party. You could draw a really cool picture of me jumping over a cow."

Pete nailed Eliza Collins in the left calf. That was a mistake. She came marching over with the Nerf football, held it up to Pete's face, and ripped it into little pieces. Then she dropped them over Pete's head like confetti.

"You can get back to your game now," she said.

Pete decided to think that was hilarious, since his other choice would have been to be embarrassed. "You kill me, Eliza!" he guffawed.

"Maybe one day," she said. Then she walked away, trailed by the Elizettes.

Pete was about to say something back to her until he realized this was a battle he couldn't win, and so he finally turned his attention to me. "You want me to draw what?"

"A picture of me jumping over a cow."

He pondered that.

"Fully clothed," I added.

"Forget it," Pete said. "Naked or nothing."

"Come on, dude. You know I can't do the naked part. But this party is going to be so fun! Food and girls and dancing and stuff. And tons of cupcakes."

Pete raised his eyebrows. He had a weakness for cupcakes. "Chocolate?"

"Double chocolate."

He sighed. "Okay, fine. One picture of you jumping over a cow coming up. Just make sure there's extra frosting."

"Awesome!"

I tried to high-five him, but Pete already had bigger things on his mind. "Wanna go find a tennis ball and whip it at Eliza's butt?"

"Nah." I was ready to return to a detention-free zone, which basically was anywhere Pete wasn't.

As I walked away he called to me, "So you're really going to go through with this party?"

"Yup. It's going to be so cool. Seriously."

"If you say so," Pete said, shaking his head. "Jumping over a cow? It seems pretty crazy."

Uh-oh.

When Pete calls something crazy, there's a pretty good chance it's crazy.

39

I should probably tell you now why I
didn't think it was crazy.

First of all, I wasn't going to get a real cow. I was going
to get a moose. Meaning, my dog Moose. He's practically
as big as a cow. And he's such a good dog that he doesn't
mind it when you drape things over his back, things like a
towel, or a blanket, or a person.

So my plan was to dress Moose up like a cow. Shouldn't
be too hard, right? Just get a white sheet, draw some huge
black circles on it with a magic marker, and we're good to
go. Oh, and borrow the cowbell from Timmy's drum set.
It'll work great.

Kids weren't going to care if it was a real cow or not
anyway, as long as the food was good.

Second of all, my sister Megan is one of the most responsible people I know. She doesn't drink or smoke or do
any of that bad stuff, and she was going to make sure the
house didn't get destroyed or anything. I just had to make
sure she remembered agreeing to have the party. Which
she didn't exactly do, but she won't remember that.

Third of all, all parents want their kids to be popular.

They'll let them go to anything, and they'll write a check for anything, as long as it means their kids are with other kids and won't be left out.

The next thing I had to do was talk to the other most responsible people I knew and make sure they were coming, too.

I started with Nareem. It took some convincing to get him on board.

His first reaction was to say, "I'm not sure I can come to a party that your parents don't even know about," as we sat in study hall and I watched him do math homework that was about five grade levels above me.

"Come on, Nareem, I need you there."

He squinted at me. "Why? Because I'm the stereotypical Indian kid who does well in school and never gets in trouble, and you need someone like that to prove that your party won't be some wild, out-of-control event?"

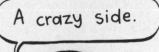

A crazy side.

There was only one answer to that question. "Yes," I said.

Nareem sighed. "Well, I appreciate your honesty. And yes, fine, I will attend your party. But you should know that there is another side to my personality."

"What kind of side is that?"

He opened his eyes wide and leaned in close to me. "A crazy side," he whispered. He looked convincing, but hey, this was Nareem we were talking about. I didn't believe him.

I should have.

My next stop was Katie Friedman.

Here, I'll let her tell you about it.

41

At first, I didn't want any part of Charlie Joe's ridiculous cow-jumping, money-making, check-collecting scheme. I swear I didn't. I was fine with his dog-walking escapade, and that ended badly enough, but thankfully no one got hurt. Not even the gopher. But this time, I was drawing the line. This time, no matter what he said, I wasn't getting involved. I really meant it.

Until like a week later.

Which is when he came up to me at school after lunch.

"Hey, Katie."

I didn't even look up. "I'm sorry, have we met?"

Charlie Joe laughed. "Yes, we've met. We met in first grade, I think, and we've been very good friends ever since."

I stuck out my hand to shake. "Katie Friedman, nice to meet you. Now leave me alone, because I don't want any part of what you're here to talk to me about."

"Come on, Katie."

I finally looked at him. "Come on what? Come on, help you out with another crazy idea, even though the last time, you blamed me when it went wrong? Come on, you need another favor from me, even though I've told you ten times I don't want to get involved?"

He nodded. "Exactly."

I rolled my eyes. "You are unbelievable."

"Thanks," Charlie Joe said, failing to detect my sarcasm. So typical.

I slid over on the bench. "You can sit down, but you can't talk about cows."

Charlie Joe smiled as if he were Santa Claus and I was a five-year-old girl who still believed. "Really? Because I have this awesome idea that's going to totally change your mind about this whole thing."

There's only one word for people like Charlie Joe: *relentless*.

"So the party is really starting to come together," Charlie Joe continued. "Pete is designing the invitation, Megan and her boyfriend are going to chaperone, the food's going to be awesome. I'm just missing one thing."

"What's that?" I asked, with a little tingle in my stomach, because I started to realize what he was getting at.

"A band."

Yes.

"A band?" I repeated, trying not to sound too excited.

"Yup," said Charlie Joe, "a band. Which is where you come in. I want to hire CHICKMATE to be the band at my party. I'll pay you, too."

Do you know how confusing it can be when a boy who's been driving you crazy for years with his ridiculous schemes suddenly has an idea that makes you incredibly happy?

I think I've told you already how much I love being in CHICKMATE. And at Jake's bar mitzvah, I discovered that playing in front of a live audience was pretty much the greatest feeling in the whole world. The chance to get to do it again—and for money!—was definitely too good to be true.

I tried to play it cool. "Well, that's a very nice and generous offer, Charlie Joe. Let me talk it over with the rest of the band and get back to you."

"Get back to me? You're kidding, right? I said I'll pay you to play at my party! Who wouldn't want to do that?"

He had a point.

"Well, it does sound like a wonderful opportunity," I said, my coolness wavering. "But I can't say yes for sure until I talk to the other girls. We're a democracy."

"Okay, fine," said Charlie Joe, "but you and your democracy let me know by tomorrow morning, or I'm just going to play music off the computer and do it that way."

Ack! I couldn't let that happen.

"Oh, what the heck. I know what they'll say. We're in. Thanks for the offer, Charlie Joe."

Charlie Joe hugged me. "I knew it! When you're big and famous and touring the world, never forget that Charlie Joe Jackson was the one who gave you your big break."

I didn't want him to think I completely endorsed his

crazy party, so I only kind of hugged him back, saying, "It'll be really fun." And then, momentarily losing my mind, I added, "And you don't have to pay us, don't worry about it."

He looked totally thrilled. "For real?! You are the most awesome person ever created!" Then he hugged me again and ran off, probably to tell his friends that he just suckered Katie Friedman into playing at his party for free.

Why am I such a good person? What is wrong with me?

Thank you, Katie Friedman, for announcing to the world what an incredibly good person you are.

Just because it's true, doesn't mean you get to put it in a book.

I would never do something like that.

Claire and James Jackson
Request the pleasure of
your company
when their son
Charles Joseph Jackson

BECOMES A MAN

Saturday, April 27th
6:00 p.m. ceremony
7:00 - 9:00 celebration
27 Almond Drive, Eastport

RSVP directly to Charlie Joe
at school only.

No gifts please.

CHARLIE JOE BECOMES A MAN

What do you think? Pretty good, right? Na-reem helped me write it.

Telling people to RSVP directly to me in school was a little risky, but it was the only way to do it. I couldn't have my mailbox at home start filling up with strange little envelopes addressed to me—my parents would have noticed that for sure.

Oh, and "no gifts please" is code for "checks only."

Did I mention I invited Zoe, too?

After Jake's bar mitzvah, we didn't talk or text or anything for a while. Or more specifically, she didn't text me, and I was too shy to text her first. (I'm pretty shy sometimes. No, seriously, I am.) I was starting to think the whole thing never happened, and I was raising all this money for nothing.

Then, about a week later, I got a text from her:

Leaving for Ohio in three weeks. did you ever ask your parents about visiting?

I texted back:

Yes—Looking good! Fingers crossed!

She texted back:

YAY!!!

So we were definitely back on texting terms, complete with exclamation points!

Anyway, I didn't necessarily want to tell her that I was throwing a party to make money just to visit her, but I did want to invite her. And I really wanted her to come. But I wanted it to sound casual. So I texted her again:

I'm having a party the week before

you go, do you want to come? Katie's
band is playing.

That way, it seemed more like I was inviting her to come
see Katie's band, not to come to my party just to see me.

She texted back:

I would love to!!!

I texted back:

Great!

She texted back:

Can't wait 2 see u! Tell katie I
say hi!

When I told Katie that Zoe said hi, she said to say hi
back. But when I started to tell her about the rest of our
text exchange, Katie waved me away. "I've got way more
interesting things to do than listen to every detail of your
love life."

"Oh, right," I said, but inside a part of me was thinking,
What could possibly be more interesting than my love life?

The party was two days away when I got the scare of my life.

We were sitting at dinner when all of a sudden Dad said, "I'm thinking of bailing on this whole college reunion thing. It's just going to be a bunch of people talking about how awesome their lives turned out, how much money they've made, and how gorgeous and perfect their kids are."

I dropped my fork.

Megan played it cooler. "Are you saying we're not gorgeous and perfect, Daddy?"

"Of course he's not saying that, honey," my mom chimed in. "You know how Dad hates show-off-y types, that's all."

I had to say something. "Well, Timmy's parents just went to his mom's college reunion, and they said they had the most amazing time in their lives."

"Really?" Mom asked. "I'm surprised Rose didn't tell me about that."

(I didn't say I had to say something *true*. I just said I had to say something.)

"I don't know," Dad said, leaning back in his chair and undoing his belt, which was a sign he was finished eating.

"I'm really only in touch with about five people from college. It might just be too weird seeing everybody else."

Just as I felt the first beads of sweat start breaking out on my forehead, my mom saved the day. "Of course we're going to go, Jim," she said. "These kinds of things come along once every ten years. It'll be a hoot!" My mom has a tendency to use phrases that haven't been popular since before I was born, like "It'll be a hoot!" and "Oh, goodness me!"

Dad got up. "We'll see." He started making his typical lame attempt at clearing the dishes, which usually ended after about one glass. Then he looked at Megan and me and said, "I'm not thrilled at the idea of leaving you guys here by yourselves for the weekend, either."

That was new. Usually it was Mom who was the nervous parent. It was obvious he was just looking for a way to get out of going to his reunion.

"Sorry, Dad, that's not gonna fly," I said. "Don't try to make excuses. You're going to that reunion. Megan and I are going to spend the whole weekend doing fun activities like weeding and dusting and going to the library."

"I love weeding," Megan said.

"And I love dusting," I added. I wanted to say I loved going to the library, too, but I couldn't quite spit it out, even as a joke.

"Enough, you two," said Mom. "Keep it up, and I'll call

your grandmother to come stay with you." That we didn't need. We loved Grandma, but she had the unfortunate habit of playing the television all day long, loud enough for people in Borneo to hear it.

(Anyone know where Borneo is? I don't. But it's a cool name for a country.)

✳ ✳ ✳

Later that night, I went to Megan's room for some last-minute planning. She was sitting in front of her giant mirror, combing her hair.

I sat down on her bed. "Everything ready on your end?"

She didn't take her eyes off her reflection. "I can't believe I let you talk me into this. I can't believe I said yes."

It didn't seem like a good time to remind her that she had never actually technically said yes, so I tried to change the subject. "Why do you comb your hair before bed, anyway? Are you trying to make sure you look good in your dreams?"

She changed the subject back. "What do you mean, is everything ready on my end? I'm not having anyone over except Willy, who's coming just to help me keep you in line."

"I love Willy!" I said, trying to keep things happy. "He's like my favorite of all the boyfriends you've ever had."

"That's nice. Charlie Joe, I really need to make sure you know what you're doing with this party. How many kids are coming, anyway?"

I didn't really want to go into details. It turned out that a lot of people were interested in cow jumping. I handed out about forty invitations, and thirty-six kids said yes.

"A bunch," I said.

"A bunch?" Megan repeated.

"A lot," I clarified.

Megan shook her head. "Seriously? And a live band? This is insane. We better hope the cops don't come."

Cops? Insane? Suddenly I was getting a little freaked out. "It's going to be a really short party," I said. "Over by nine o'clock. What could happen?"

"Life," Megan said, still combing. "Life could happen."

Oh, yeah. Life.

Let's party.

Charlie Joe's Financial Tip #7

DO AS LITTLE WORK AS POSSIBLE. BUT DON'T DO SO LITTLE THAT IT ENDS UP MAKING *EXTRA* WORK.

I'm not going to sit here and say you never have to work in your life. That would just be dumb. Everyone knows you have to do *some* work to get by. So don't be so concerned with doing *no* work that you end up doing *more* work. (Advice I myself have ignored, by the way, more than once or twice.)

Like say you're cleaning some dishes, and you rinse a glass but you're too lazy to dry it, and because it's still wet it slips out of your hand and crashes to the floor. Now you have to get the dustpan and broom and clean up a bunch of broken glass.

Way more work.

Or say your best friend asks you to do something, and you really don't want to do it, because it feels like work. If you don't do it, you'll spend tons of time trying to make up some sort of excuse, and tons of time trying to admit you were wrong without actually apologizing, and

the next thing you know, you realize it would have been a heck of a lot less work doing the thing in the first place.

So do as little work as you can. But remember, sometimes no work actually means more work.

Part Five
THE UH AND THE OH

46

The party got off to a great start.

By 6:20 p.m., I had already made $862.00.

It was incredible: after a kid got dropped off, he or she would come straight over to me and hand me a check. I would hug (girl) or high-five (boy) them, thank them, and point them toward the food.

We'd turned the garage, driveway, and backyard into the party zone. The band was set up in the garage, the driveway was going to be the dance floor, and all the food and drinks and some chairs and stuff were in the backyard. Megan and Willy had bought tons of pizzas, snacks, cookies, and sodas. She also had to buy paper plates and cups and napkins and stuff. (She said I owed her about two hundred bucks for all of it. Would it be considered rude or ungrateful to ask to see the receipt?)

At first, people were happy just eating, drinking, and hanging out. Katie's band was playing some weird music as a warm-up. (Pete Milano was pretending to dance to it by jumping around like an epileptic baboon, but Phil Manning and Celia Barbarossa were slow dancing like it was some big romantic song or something.)

When the band took a break, I asked Katie what kind

of music they were playing. She said it was inspired by Ethiopian tribal chants.

"I don't get it," I said.

She did the classic eye-roll. "The cow-jumping ceremony? It comes from Ethiopia?"

"Oh, right." Oops.

"Where's Zoe?" Katie asked.

"Who?" I said, acting like I had completely not even noticed that Zoe hadn't shown up yet.

"Zoe? Remember her? The whole reason you're jumping over a cow?"

"Oh, her. Well, she'll get here when she gets here."

"Right," Katie said, not buying my casual act for a second.

As she started up the music again I asked, "Do you guys know any Beatles?" but she was already midchant and didn't hear me.

✳ ✳ ✳

At 6:45, I went inside to make sure everything was ready for the big moment.

The first thing I saw was a cow in our kitchen.

Let me explain: about a week earlier I'd told Mark Lichtman, whose dad owned a house-painting company, that I'd give him twenty dollars if he could make a plain white sheet look like the back of a cow. He'd done an amazing job—the black spots looked incredibly real. Then Megan cut holes in the sheet for the head and the legs, and stapled the bottom together so it made like a kind of smock.

Now Moose was wearing it, and it fit perfectly. The cowbell tied around his neck sealed the deal.

I figured that considering it was pretty dark outside, he could definitely pass as a cow.

Moose was wagging his tail, perfectly happy with his new outfit, but Coco was acting weird. Either she was jealous, or had a thing against cows, but she was barking and running in circles around Moose. I decided to distract her with a couple of chewy snacks, which worked for the six seconds it took for her to eat them. Then it was back to the barking and the running.

Nareem came in. "Are you ready to commence the big performance? It's time." He was jiggling his feet nervously, with a candy bar in one hand and a cup of grape soda in the other.

"Are you okay?" I asked.

"I'm fine," he said, but he didn't sound fine. I figured he was just a little nervous since he was going to introduce me.

We took Moose outside and led him to the small area in the backyard where he liked to nap. Immediately, people started murmuring.

"Hey, that's a dog," Gina Green said.

"I thought this was a cow jumping," added Lily Romann.

"Are you jumping over a dog?" asked Bill Winston.

"Who cares?" said Pete, coming through in the clutch. "Dog, cow, whatever, as long as the cupcakes are fresh."

"I WOULD LIKE THE AUDIENCE TO PLEASE BE QUIET!" Nareem shouted. That shut everyone up. None of us had ever heard Nareem raise his voice above a very polite and gentle murmur. He looked around, pleased with himself, although his legs were still going a mile a minute. "Ladies and gentlemen, if I could have your attention, please. It is true; this is not a cow. This is Charlie Joe's dog, Moose. However, Charlie Joe has done his research, and he has been assured by the proper authorities that for this kind of ceremony, if you are not able to pro-cure the services of an actual cow, then a dog will suf-fice, provided it is dressed up to resemble a cow." (My research, by the way, had involved asking Timmy what he thought, and Timmy saying he thought using Moose was a great idea.)

"BOOOO!" yelled a bunch of kids, but they were kid-ding around. I hoped.

Nareem looked at me nervously, and I gestured for him to keep going. "We are gathered here tonight to bear wit-ness as Charlie Joe Jackson, in keeping with the ancient Hamar tradition, becomes a man by jumping over a cow. Or, in this case, a dog."

Moose picked this moment to decide he was sleepy, and so he lay down and began to nap.

"Hey, doesn't he have to be standing up?" some kid asked.

"Yeah," some other kid answered. "Otherwise, what's the point? Anyone can jump over a sleeping dog."

I realized we had to make this happen, and make it happen quick, so that we could get people back to the stuff they liked: food, music, dancing, and hanging out with the opposite sex without parents around.

I had prepared a short speech, and I asked Katie for her microphone. "Thank you all for coming," I said. "This is a very important and meaningful day for me. I have watched so many of you go through bar mitzvahs, confirmations, and other ceremonies, and I'm so happy to finally have the chance to participate in my own special ritual." I raised my glass of cream soda, and everyone else raised their own glasses. "Tonight I become a man."

I pointed to Katie, and she cued the band. The plan was for her to play "Jump" by Van Halen, and right at the beginning of the first chorus I would sprint forward and jump over my cow-dog.

She was just finishing the intro section of the song when the music stopped.

And the lights went out.

And the power went out.

And the party went south.

After the power went out, nobody said anything for about ten seconds, until Becca from Katie's band shouted, "I think we blew a fuse."

Everybody looked at each other. Then everybody looked at me. I wasn't sure what to do. Should I go through with the jump? Should I try to fix the power? Should I admit to everybody that I had no idea how to fix the power?

I was standing there trying to figure out my next move when I heard a voice say, "I got this." It was Willy, Megan's boyfriend. He and Megan were heading toward the house. I ran over to them.

"You guys know what to do?" I asked.

Willy put his arm around me. "Yeah, I'm sure it's just a circuit breaker, shouldn't be a big deal. We can't let a little blown fuse get in the way of the big night, am I right?"

I could have kissed him right then. I knew that was Megan's job, but still.

We went into the furnace room, which was where the circuit breaker box thingie was. By then it was about 7:00, still pretty light outside, but not a lot of light in the basement.

Willy looked at us. "You guys know where a flash-light is?"

Megan and I shook our heads.

"A lantern? Penlight? Anything?"

More shaking of heads.

Willy shook his head. "Unbelievable."

Then he remembered he had a flashlight app on his phone. He opened up the fuse box and tried to read the labels, but they were in my dad's completely unreadable handwriting.

"What language is this?" Willy muttered.

"Fatherese," I said, trying to lighten the mood, but no one laughed.

Willy started flipping switches but nothing happened.

Just then Timmy came running in. "What's happening? Everyone wants to know what's going on. Also, we need more root beer."

Katie followed thirty seconds later. She put her hand on my shoulder. "Sorry bout that. Were we playing too loud?"

"Of course not," I said.

"Nothing but Beatles for the rest of the night," she said, which made me feel a little better.

Willy kept fiddling while we all watched. Then he said, "Wait, I think this must be it," and he flipped one last switch.

The power came back on!

We all cheered and hugged each other and slapped Willy on the back. For the second time in less than five minutes, I felt like kissing him. Timmy and I got some more root beer from the fridge, and everyone headed back outside, ready to get on with the big show.

By the time we got to the garage, we could hear some strange sounds coming from outside. Sounds that sounded like human screaming.

When we got outside, we saw the strangest thing.

It was raining in the backyard. On a perfectly clear night. And everyone was getting soaked.

Then a siren started blaring, like the kind you hear in movies when a city is about to get bombed.

As we covered our ears and dodged the raindrops, Megan yelled, "Uh-oh." Willy yelled something much worse. And Katie, Timmy, and I just stood there and tried to understand what was happening.

When Willy turned to Megan and said, "I wish your

Dad didn't have such bad handwriting," I suddenly got it. He hadn't just turned the lights back on. He turned *everything* back on.

The lights, the outdoor sprinkler system, the security alarm.

Everything.

✳ ✳ ✳

For a second no one said anything.

Then it was complete craziness.

Everyone started yelling, running around, crashing into each other, spilling food, spilling drinks, slipping on spilled drinks, falling down, getting up again, and falling down again.

Phil Manning took off his shirt to remind everybody that he was the strongest kid in the grade.

Celia Barbarossa hugged Phil to remind everyone that she was going out with the strongest kid in the grade.

Eric Clumpsty and Mark Lichtman decided to see if they could scream louder than the siren, until Eric dissolved in a coughing fit, which ended only when Evan Wilson gave him the Heimlich.

Eliza Collins and the Elizettes ran around screaming "Ew," even though there's absolutely nothing gross about being drenched with water. Annoying, yes. Gross, no.

And Pete Milano grabbed a plastic tablecloth, threw it

on the ground, splashed water on it, and turned it into a Slip 'n Slide. With a mouthful of cupcakes, he let out a banshee wail and slid down the tablecloth, landing head-first in a rose bush. "Yes!" he screamed, picking thorns out of his face.

Say what you will about Pete, he knows how to make the best of a bad situation.

Almost everyone was soaking wet. I saw cell phones coming out—kids calling their parents to come and pick them up. Then one girl started crying because her cell phone was ruined—I think it was Margaret Petlow, whose main claim to fame was wearing sweaters every day of the year, even when it was boiling-hot out.

Now she'd be famous for being the first one to cry at my Cow Jump.

Coco, meanwhile, decided that Moose should not be a

cow anymore. She wanted him out of that costume right that very second. She tried to rip it off him with her teeth, which Moose did not appreciate. They started chasing each other, and Coco plowed into the drinks table, sending cups of Mountain Dew and Dr Pepper flying into the air and landing on people's heads. Coco finally caught up to Moose, and he allowed her to de-cow him. They sniffed and made up. But Moose was definitely still a little shaken up.

I could tell because he walked up to Hannah Spivero and peed on her leg.

Hannah looked down, kind of shocked. Jake yelled, "Hey!" and Moose ran away, knocking over Becca Clausen, the five-foot-nine soccer player and guitarist, who had wandered over to see if she could help. Becca looked kind of shocked. I don't think she'd ever been knocked over before.

Meanwhile Hannah, who was wet and dirty and had

dog pee on her leg, ran over to Moose and hugged him. "It's not your fault, Moosie," she said. "I still love you."

I almost fell right back in love with her that very moment. But I was too busy wondering what would go wrong next.

I didn't have to wait long.

Out of the corner of my eye I saw this blurry shape sprinting like a crazy person. I turned my head to see him coming right toward me.

"I WILL JUMP THE COW! I WILL JUMP THE COW!"

It was Nareem.

Remember when Nareem said he had a "crazy side?" It turns out that his crazy side comes out to play when he has a lot of sugar. And it turns out that seven cupcakes, four snickers bars, twelve chocolate chip cookies, and nine cups of grape soda qualifies as a lot of sugar.

Which explains why he had decided that *someone* had to jump the cow, and that someone had to be him.

Oh, I almost forgot to mention—for some reason Nareem decided that I was the cow.

Everyone looked up from ducking the sprinklers and running for shelter to watch this lunatic flying at me at full speed. I ducked just as he made his leap, but I think he would have cleared me even if I had been Lebron James. I mean, he jumped HIGH. He soared over me, arms over his head, with a huge smile on his face, as everyone burst into a huge cheer. I bet it was the best moment of his life.

Too bad it was immediately followed by the worst.

Nareem was so excited to make his giant leap for mankind that he forgot to check out what was behind me. It wasn't until he was in the air, directly over my head, that he saw the glass table.

He had about .8 seconds to absorb that fact, and then . . . crash.

Actually, more like . . . CCCRRRRAAAAASH!

Some people screamed. Other people closed their eyes. Katie buried her head in her hands. Everyone held their breath.

Nareem lay there for about twenty seconds, then slowly got up. A smile slowly spread across his face. He didn't have a scratch on him. The table wasn't so lucky.

"I'm okay!" he announced. "I jumped the cow!" Then

he raised his arms to the sky and shouted it to the world. "TONIGHT I BECAME A MAN!"

Katie marched up to her boyfriend and looked at him like he'd just grown a second head. "You are definitely not a man," she snapped. "You are a crazy idiot who could have just killed himself!"

Nareem's smile wavered for just a second. "I jumped the cow," he reminded Katie, a little less confidently.

"Nareem's definitely a man!" Pete confirmed. He started chanting "NAREEM! NAREEM! NAREEM!" and soon everyone joined in. "NAREEM! NAREEM! NAREEM!" Nareem went all over the yard, accepting high-fives and congratulations from his new fans, as Katie stared at him as if seeing him for the first time.

Then, somewhere around the tenth "NAREEM!" the sprinklers turned off.

And then the alarm turned off.

Everybody let out a huge cheer. A small part of me wondered who managed to find all the switches, but most of me was ecstatic. We were saved! My money was still in my pocket, we weren't being rained on anymore, and I was still going to Ohio! Things were looking up!

I was just about to tell Katie to fire up the amplifiers again when I felt a tap on my shoulder.

It was a familiar tap.

Horribly familiar.

I turned around and looked directly into the faces of my mother and father.

Megan was right behind them, her face the color of red licorice.

My parents looked around for about a minute, taking it all in—the drenched kids, the broken glass, the scattered instruments, the mangled bushes, the ripped plates, the spilled cups, the soaked chips, the waterlogged dogs (one with part of a cow costume still on his back), the destroyed grass, and the tall Indian boy who had just become a man.

My mom sat down in shock. My dad looked at me and smiled the nicest, kindest, most insincere smile in the world.

"I'm sure there's a perfectly reasonable explanation for all of this," he said.

48

It turns out it was all Fred Semple's fault.

You don't know who Fred Semple is? Well, I'll tell you. He's the guy who went to my dad's reunion just to tell everyone how awesome he was. The guy who told my parents that he sold his hedge fund when he was forty to sail around the world with his boat and his captain and his chef and his second wife who was super hot. The guy whose behavior proved to my mom that my dad was right, that the reunion was just a bunch of people bragging and showing off and pretending to care about other people's family pictures.

And he's the guy that ultimately made my parents decide to leave the reunion early and come back home just in
time to see their backyard turned into an unlicensed water
park.

Thanks, Fred Semple.

I hope your boat hits an iceberg.

49

As the kids were getting picked up by their very confused parents, Megan, Willy, and I tried to put the house back together as best we could. Katie and her band packed up. And Nareem came down from his crazy sugar rush.

"I'm so terribly sorry about your table," he said to my parents, "but it would be disingenuous for me to say that I regret what I did."

I had no idea what *disingenuous* meant, but my mom seemed to buy it, because she brought him a hot cup of tea.

My dad sat on the porch just watching us clean up, not saying a word. Moose and Coco slept peacefully at his feet. My mom tried to not help us—which was hard for her—but she did insist on sweeping up all the broken glass.

While we were cleaning up, Megan and I discussed our next move. We decided that instead of trying to make something up, we would tell my parents the truth. I figured that the only way for them to understand anything, and possibly not kill me, was to admit everything.

I was just about to launch into my long explanation when guess who showed up?

Zoe.

"I'm so sorry I'm late!" she said, jumping out of her mom's car. "But I know you won't be mad when I tell you my amazing news!" It took her about five seconds to realize that the party wasn't exactly going as planned. "Wait. What's wrong?"

My dad smiled at her. "What makes you think something's wrong?" he said.

"It's kind of complicated," I told Zoe. So I ended up telling the whole story to her and my parents at the same time: about how my parents said I had to make my own money to go visit her in Ohio, so I decided to have my own bar mitzvah, and how Megan helped me plan it because she was a great sister, not because she was a bad daughter, and then I told them all about the ancient Ethiopian Hamar tradition of cow jumping, and dressing Moose up like a cow, and hiring Katie's band, and collecting the checks, and blowing a fuse, and Willy trying to fix it, and the sprinklers going off, and the alarm going off, and Coco freaking out at Moose, and Moose peeing on Hannah, and Pete creating a Slip 'n Slide, and Nareem jumping over me and crashing into the table.

It sounds like a long story, but I told it pretty fast. I think I just wanted to get it over with. The whole thing took like nine seconds.

Finally my dad said one word: "Wow." Then he added, "Even for you, Charlie Joe. Wow."

My mom, as usual, was focused on our guest. "Charlie

Joe, we'll discuss all this later," she said. "But first, Zoe, you said you had some amazing news, and we could all use some right about now."

"Oh, boy," Zoe said. "Oh, boy. Oh, boy. Oh boy."

"That's a weird introduction to great news," I said. I think some part of me knew what she was going to say before she said it.

Zoe looked embarrassed. "Oh, Charlie Joe, now I feel bad that you went through all this trouble! The thing is, it turns out we're not moving to Ohio after all. My parents didn't want to make me go to a new school again, so my grandparents decided to move to Kenwood instead." She tried to smile. "So I'll only be twenty minutes away. Isn't that great?"

O.

M.

G.

The last couple of weeks went through my head—Jake's bar mitzvah, seeing Zoe again only to find out she was moving again, taking my dad's dare to pay my own way to Ohio, and thinking I could get away with throwing myself a cow-jumping party as a money-making scheme.

All for a girl who wasn't even moving away after all.

Suddenly I felt like an idiot—as so of course, instead of getting mad at myself, I got mad at Zoe.

"What do you mean you're not going?" I said. "I

probably just got grounded for life making money to go visit you!"

Zoe's face fell. "I'm sorry, Charlie Joe. I thought you would be happy."

I finally lost my cool. "DO I LOOK HAPPY?"

Zoe jumped back like she'd been smacked. I thought she might burst into tears, but before she did, she ran back to her mom's car, and they drove away.

I just stood there and watched her go. I felt angry, ridiculous, and most of all, guilty.

My dad walked over and put his hand on my shoulder.

"You're not going to be grounded for life," he said. "Just most of it."

Charlie Joe's Financial Tip #8

EMOTIONAL WORK IS STILL WORK.

Work isn't always just a job, or homework, or chores.

Sometimes it's emotional.

Like, when you do something special for a girl you think you like, but it turns out to be the craziest idea you ever had, and you have to figure out a way to make your parents not hate you forever.

That's a lot of work.

Life is hard enough as it is, and it's filled with work. Yard work, schoolwork, actual work-for-a-living work. Try to avoid the emotional work if at all possible.

I ended up grounded "for the foreseeable future," was how my dad put it. It was pretty painful, but it wasn't the end of the world. My parents also said I had to get a different kind of job—a volunteer job that served the community. I was in no position to argue.

"Sometimes I just don't understand you, Charlie Joe," my mom said later that night, as they told me the punishment. "Did you really think you were going to get away with this? Nareem could have gotten seriously hurt! And even if nothing went wrong, and we didn't come home until tomorrow, don't you realize that the neighbors would have told us that while we were gone, twenty middle school kids were running around having a party at my house?"

It was more like thirty middle school students, but I wasn't about to point that out.

"And, Megan, what were you thinking?" Mom went on. "This is not like you. Not like you at all." Megan stared at the ground and didn't say anything. Meanwhile, Will looked like he thought my dad was going to spank him.

"Megan was just helping me," I said. "You can't punish her." Megan glanced at me and smiled a tiny smile.

"No car privileges for a month," my dad announced to Megan, which made her smile disappear pretty quickly.

My mom shook her head. "Well, Charlie Joe, I'm glad you told us the truth. You made some very bad decisions, but I'm glad you told us the truth."

"Thanks, Mom," I said. "I'm glad I did, too."

"One last thing," said my dad, bringing over his laptop. "Since you seem so interested in Ethiopia, we wanted to show you something."

He went to YouTube and played a video called "Endless Famine—Ethiopia." It was shocking, intense, and really sad. There are a lot of children there who don't have enough to eat. They were really skinny, way too skinny. Some were crying.

Soon I was crying.

"I am so, so sorry," I said. "I was greedy and stupid and wrong."

My parents hugged me.

"No argument from me," said my dad.

My mom gave me an extra hug. "Now about that money," she said. We clicked a few more buttons and donated everything I made from my cow-jumping party to an Ethiopian Relief Fund.

That made me feel a little bit less like a selfish jerk.

A little.

I'm still a little emotional from that last part, so I'll let Katie tell you what happened next.

52

First of all, in terms of Charlie Joe's cow-jumping party? I thought it was pretty amazing.

But that's easy for me to say. I'm not the one who got grounded for almost life.

So the next day, when he called me to talk about it, I tried to make him feel better. "Charlie Joe, you created an event that people will be talking about FOREVER. That's a real accomplishment."

He took a deep breath into the phone. "Yeah, but I still feel stupid. Life isn't all about money, you know."

"Uh, yeah, I do know," I said.

"Plus, I think Zoe must hate me now."

"Wait, why do you think that?"

"Because I'm a big jerk, that's why." Then he told me the story of yelling at her in his driveway, which did sound pretty darn jerky.

"I'm sure she'll forgive you," I said.

"I doubt it. I wouldn't forgive me if I were her."

I had never heard Charlie Joe sound this down before, and I didn't like it. For some reason, I preferred him cocky and obnoxious. So I decided to take action. "Well, that's just crazy, and I'm sure you're wrong, but there's only one way to find out. Let's call her."

Charlie Joe paused, then said, "You mean now?"

"Yup, I mean now. I'm conferencing her in."

"Oh, boy."

I put Charlie Joe on hold and dialed Zoe.

"Katie?"

I added Charlie Joe to the call. "Hey, Zoe, it's me with Charlie Joe."

"Hi, Zoe," said Charlie Joe.

"Hey," she answered, clearly not in a very forgiving mood.

"So, I wanted to say I'm sorry," Charlie Joe began. "I acted like a jerk yesterday. I hope you're not still mad."

"I am still mad," Zoe said, clearing up any confusion.

There was an awkward moment of silence before Charlie Joe spoke again. "Well, I'm really glad that you aren't moving to Ohio."

Someone took a deep breath, and I was pretty sure it was Zoe. "Charlie Joe, it was really fun to see you at Jake's bar mitzvah, but it's probably stupid to think we could ever go out or anything, living in different towns."

"Oh," Charlie Joe said. "Um . . . okay."

Suddenly I felt that old feeling of wanting to help Charlie Joe out. It's annoying, the way it keeps coming back. Like a rash.

"Zoe, Charlie Joe really likes you," I said. "In fact, he went to a lot of trouble coming up with this crazy idea, trying to raise the money to go visit you."

"Not that crazy," said Charlie Joe, trying to bounce back.

"Charlie Joe, I really like you, too," Zoe said. "You're awesome. We can definitely stay in touch and text and stuff. And maybe in high school we can hang out or something. But right now, it just seems like we should just be friends. Right?"

This time, the deep breath was Charlie Joe's. "I guess."

"But thank you, Charlie Joe," said Zoe. "Thank you for throwing that party just so you could come see me. That's pretty much the sweetest thing anybody has ever done for me. And from what I hear, it was completely awesome."

"It was," Charlie Joe said, the familiar swagger back in his voice. "There's never been another party like it."

Zoe laughed, and I smiled to myself, thinking, *It's good to have him back.*

53

I think charlie Joe wants to tell you the rest of the story.

54

It's true, I do.

In school the next week, everybody talked about the party for about two days straight. The only person who was able to change the subject was Eliza Collins, by showing off her latest new gadget.

"It's called the Phonetastic," she announced, holding up this large, strange-looking contraption. "It's a combination phone/lipstick holder/compact mirror/hairbrush/iron. And the best part is it tells you when you're done."

She pushed a button and an actual hairbrush shot out of the phone and she started brushing her hair. After about ten seconds, a voice from the phone announced, "Hair looks perfect."

Everybody *ooh*-ed and *aah*-ed.

"You know," I said, "with the money you spent on that stupid phone, you could feed a family in Africa for a year."

Everybody turned and looked at me.

"What?" I said. "It's true."

"Well, Charlie Joe," said Eliza, "it just so happens I'm donating my Botman to charity."

"Really?" Hannah Spivero asked.

"Which charity?" Nareem wanted to know.

Eliza made this scrunched-up face that she used

whenever she wanted to convince someone she was thinking hard about something. "Um, one of the ones where the people really need robots."

"I need a robot," Pete Milano moaned. "Pick me! Pick me!"

Soon everyone was yelling, "Pick me!" and "Can I have it?" and "I'll be your best friend!" and "I'm totally a charity case!"

Not everyone could be as enlightened as me, I guess.

Somewhere in the middle of my third week of grounded-ness, I was coming back to the house after walking the dogs when I saw my mom and Katie Friedman having a conversation in the backyard—right about at the spot where Nareem Ramdal crashed into the glass table.

"Katie has a great idea," my mom announced.

Katie smiled. "I know it's you who usually has the ideas, Charlie Joe, but seeing as how that hasn't been working out so great for you lately, I thought I'd come up with one of my own."

"I love ideas," I said. "Lay it on me."

Katie pulled a pamphlet out of her back pocket. "Well, I know how you need to get a volunteer job, and I thought it might be a good idea for you to try the library."

I kind of laughed and choked at the same time.

My mom glared at me. "Just listen."

I glared back. "Fine."

Katie handed me the pamphlet. "Well, it's actually really kind of fun. The people there are really nice, and there are tons of books to read during your down time." She raised her eyebrows. "We all know how much you love books."

I didn't smile back.

"Plus, you get free chocolate chip cookies at the café," she added.

I shrugged. "I don't know," I said. Then looking for an exit strategy I added, "I think the dogs need some water."

As I started to walk inside, I heard Katie call after me. "And you'd get to work with me."

I turned back around.

Katie was smiling at me.

It was a new kind of smile.

The kind that might be a little more than just, *I'm smiling at one of my oldest friends.*

I walked back over to Katie, as my mom quietly took the dogs and led them into the house.

"Okay," I said. "Let's try it."

* * *

Two days later, I was surrounded by books of all shapes and sizes. There were books everywhere. Books, books, books. Me, and a building full of books.

But for some reason, I liked it.

Who would've thought?

"Did you ever think you'd be sitting in the middle of a

library actually enjoying yourself?" Katie said, reading my mind as usual.

"My reputation is ruined," I answered.

We were on break, finishing up about forty cookies, all washed down by delicious, ice-cold chocolate milk.

"Hey, Charlie Joe," Katie whispered. (Whispering is the only legal way to talk in the library.) "Can I tell you something?"

"Sure," I whispered back.

"I'm thinking about breaking up with Nareem."

I felt the blood start to rush to my head. "No way."

Katie nodded. "Yup."

"Why? Because he acted crazy at my party and crashed into a table?"

She shook her head. "No, that was actually pretty amazing."

"Well, why then?" I asked.

Katie shrugged. "It's just time, maybe."

That's as good a reason as any, I guess.

But I wasn't sure it was the real reason.

We looked at each other for a few seconds, not saying anything. Then I looked up and saw my supervisor, a sweet old lady named Mrs. Sixsmith, waving at me. She was pointing at a huge pile of books.

I stood up suddenly. "I better go."

"Yup," Katie said, getting up, too.

I gave her an awkward hug and went over to stack the books, which were all romantic mysteries. I happened to glance down at the title of the first book on the pile.

It was called *Some Loves Were Meant To Be.*

I smiled, shook my head, and took a deep breath.

Then I went to work.

AUTHOR'S NOTE

No dogs or cows were harmed in the making of this book.

To learn more about hunger in Africa and other places around the world, and to find out how to help, please visit savethechildren.org.

ACKNOWLEDGMENTS

I owe a huge debt to the following people: Nancy Mercado, Michele Rubin, Simon Boughton, Angus Killick, Neal Porter, Lucy Del Priore, Lauren A. Burniac, Katie Halata, Holly Hunnicut, Samantha Metzger, Molly Brouillette, Allison Verost, Andrew Arnold, Angie Chen, J. P. Coovert, Susan Cohen, Brianne Johnson, Amy Berkower, the CJJ team at Brilliance Audio, Katie Fee, Caitlin Sweeny, Tricia Tierney and everyone at Barnes and Noble Westport, Peter Glassman and everyone at Books Of Wonder, Deborah White and everyone at the Westport Public Library, the swell folks at R.J. Julia, all my colleagues at Spotco, Cathy Utz, Charlie Greenwald, Joe Greenwald, Jack Greenwald, Barbara Kellerman, Jonathan Greenwald, Kenny Greenwald, Ellen Greenwald, Jessica Greenwald, Jake Greenwald, the entire Utz extended family, everyone whom I forgot (sorry), and everyone else who will come into my writing life between now and when this book actually comes out.

And two non-people, Coco and Abby.